CUT TO THE QUICK

QUICK

Short stories for busy people

ANTHONY TALMAGE

I

CONTENTS

DEDICATION

I would like to thank all those kind readers who took the trouble to write reviews on Amazon (many rated as 5 star – thank you), of my second non-fiction book *Dowse Your Way To Psychic Power*. Here's what some of them said: 'Simply and intelligently written with great explanations and no jargon'…'I couldn't put it down until I came to the end...then I was sad I'd finished it!'…'The most interesting book on dowsing I have found so far'...'an absolute must for anyone interested in rebalancing their lives'…'Thank you, Anthony. Would love to read more in depth books by you in the future…' Many of these happy reviewers went on to read my third non-fiction book *In Tune With The Infinite Mind* which is now also helping to change people's lives.

FOREWORD

This book is a break from my usual genres – in fact it's the first short story collection I have ever published. It's in response to the many people who have said they love bite-sized fiction that will distract them for just a few minutes from their stressful routines. I've tried to come up with just such escapism, although my last story is not really bite-sized – it's more of a novella. But I thought it would fit into the general theme of a 'gallimaufry of divertissement.'

THE RIVAL

'Ever since that bitch walked into your life, you've behaved like a lovesick schoolboy,' Mabel Diprose snorted contemptuously at her husband across the breakfast table.

Percy Diprose sighed and lowered his Daily Mirror. He longed for the courage to assert himself; to stand up to his formidable wife. In his fantasies he would say, 'To Hell with your disapproval. I love Lucy and she loves me and if you can't accept it you can clear out.' But all he could think of as he withered under Mabel's gaze was, 'Don't call Lucy a bitch like that. It's...it's...not right...'

This prompted another torrent of recrimination. 'Haven't I been patient and understanding? Not complained when you've come home at all hours, put up with you spending more money on HER than me...' She had got into her stride now and Percy let the familiar litany wash over him. Percy would have been quite happy if Mabel had agreed to go their separate ways. But she would have none of it – keeping up appearances was paramount. So here they

1

were, locked in this unsatisfactory *ménage a trois*.

He should have taken his father's advice all those years ago when he'd first brought Mabel home. Old George Diprose had seen in his future daughter-in-law the seeds of a self-centred, domineering harridan.

And how accurate his instincts had been, brooded Percy. But now, all these years later, he'd found an unselfish, warm and responsive kindred spirit. And the moment had come to show himself worthy of her. It was a confrontation he'd been dreading. But, he must brace himself to his duty, as Winston Churchill had said in response to overwhelming enemy action. Lucy deserved nothing less.

'Mabel, dear, there's something I've got to tell you. It's about Lucy...'As his courage threatened to drain away, Percy drew strength from all that Lucy and he meant to each other now.

After years of marital fidelity, thought Percy, he deserved a relationship that could bring a little joy into his life. He knew it had been hard on his wife - to make this...concession...But, he must not soften now. He was going to see his new responsibilities through.

He took a deep breath and avoided Mabel's gimlet

glare. 'Lucy's...er...Lucy's pregnant...' Before his wife could react Percy plunged on, 'I don't know how it happened; I took every precaution but something went wrong...and...well... she's expecting,' he ended lamely.

Mabel Diprose struggled to keep her feelings under control and Percy waited for the tide of recriminations.

'I can't believe it. I just can't believe it,' Mabel's several chins shook with indignation. 'It was the one thing you promised. I was civilised enough to understand your...your...needs and so I turned a blind eye.

'I tolerated that bitch taking my husband over. I put up with her coming into this house and mooning over you. I thought you'd eventually get tired of going off with her at all hours. And now you've got the nerve to tell me she's going to have a...' Mabel found she couldn't finish the sentence.

Percy began reaching out a comforting hand but then withdrew it awkwardly. 'I'm really sorry dear. But...well...nature has obviously taken a hand and I must see my responsibilities through ...'

Mabel couldn't stand the thought of her husband cosseting and fussing over that creature. It was almost beyond endurance. He'd be spending even more time away from home now. And after he had promised. It was the only condition, she recalled, that she'd laid down when she'd first found out about Lucy.

She remembered being so cool and controlled. Eventually, she had asked only one thing of her husband: that he wouldn't allow any "complications" to threaten their marital routine.

She'd said that if he kept him and his...his..."obsession" in a different compartment of his life, they might make it work. And it had, after a fashion. But now this...

Later that summer, it happened while Lucy and Percy were out walking in companionable silence together. It was a glorious day and the Sussex countryside was a rolling mosaic of yellow, green and blue.

Suddenly Lucy stopped in her tracks and a flicker of pain crossed her face and she gasped. Percy knew instantly the reason - she was going into labour. 'Now whatever you do, keep calm,' he told her, feeling far from calm himself. Leading her gently back to the car he said. 'I've got all the things you might need stashed away in the boot for just this eventuality. They told me at the clinic that if this happened I was to drive you straight there and they'd take care of everything.'

He added patting her extended abdomen reassuringly, 'That's one advantage of paying for private healthcare. When the crunch comes you get personal attention.'

He assisted Lucy into the back where she had more room. 'Just take deep breaths, my darling, and we'll be there in no time.'

Minutes later he was helping her into the practice's cheerful reception. A nurse whisked Lucy through a door which led to private examination rooms.

Percy paced up and down thinking how he was acting like a typical father. Mabel would not approve, not approve at all. He smiled at the thought.

'Mr Diprose...' A hand touched his arm. A white-coated figure in his mid-thirties, a stethoscope dangling against his chest, bent close to him. 'Mr Diprose, please step into my office. It's quiet in there and we can talk.'

Percy's smile died when he saw the expression on the other man's face. 'Mr Diprose, I'm the consultant surgeon...I'm afraid there are complications...'

Percy felt himself go white and a cold fist clutched his stomach. After all Lucy and he'd been through together, was fate going to snatch their happiness away?

'What sort of complications?'

'I won't go into medical technicalities but what it amounts to is that Lucy's life's in danger. We need to operate.'

Percy nodded dumbly.

The surgeon added kindly, 'You can wait in here if you like and we'll let you know as soon as Lucy's out of the operating theatre.' He put an understanding hand on Percy's shoulder and then turned away. 'I'll get nurse to bring you a cup of tea.'

As the terrifying thought that he might lose Lucy hit him, thoughts of their first encounter tumbled through his mind. It was in that shop in the High Street where their eyes had met and Cupid's arrow had gone straight to his heart. Instantly, he'd been captivated. Mabel had been a faithful wife to him, he thought, but their relationship was all so…dull…And, he'd needed something more than she could give – a soulmate he could pour his heart out to, who didn't make him feel guilty when he failed, who'd listen to all his frustrations and disappointments without judging him. Yes, Lucy had loved him with no strings attached - just because he was Percy Diprose.

But he'd failed her. He'd allowed her to get pregnant

and now she was in mortal danger. At this moment she was fighting for her life - probably dreaming of him as the knife bit deep into her flesh. He shuddered. How could he have been so selfish? If they came through this, he resolved, everything would be different.

He didn't care what her friends said, he'd make Mabel accept Lucy. If she wouldn't, his wife could go and live with her mother permanently.

The afternoon wore on and Percy's tortured thoughts were abruptly abandoned as the door opened. The consultant stood before him but this time his expression was a mixture of triumph and relief.

'I'm delighted to tell you Mr Diprose that the operation was a complete success. Lucy withstood the trauma better than we could have hoped. Considering what she's been through, she's in excellent health...'

He held up his hand to forestall Percy's next question. 'And so's her offspring.' He smiled, 'But you really ought to have taken more effective family planning precautions you know.

'For a pedigree Golden Retriever she's produced five of the blackest mongrels...'

THE PAST IS ANOTHER COUNTRY – THEY DO THINGS DIFFERENTLY THERE

It is true that after the war resentments burned in many a chest in Guernsey over how we'd all coped under the jackboot. But it was still a surprise when two of my oldest chums squared up to each other and started staggering about the public bar of the Guernsey Flag like two senile wrestlers.

'course, during the Occupation some did better than others, if you know what I mean. When the Germans was finally kicked out, there was a flurry of officialdom.

Promises were made that collaborators would be punished. But I suppose the authorities had more important things on their minds and nothing much was done. And, in the end, we all picked up the pieces and got on with our lives.

For a few years there was the odd insult thrown in the heat of the moment - some girls who had bestowed their favours on the occupiers were called 'jerrybags.' But no-one was tarred and feathered.

So there we was, me and Raymond Le Boutillier and Ebenezer Machon, reminiscing over our pints about when we was lads in the war when Raymond accuses Ebby's dad of being a Quisling. Well, he didn't actually say Quisling, but Ebby took it that way. Before I could steer them onto safer ground they was on their feet flailing their fists at each other.

No-one was in much danger of being hurt, except Ebby and Raymond. They was like two old dinosaurs fighting under water. They was not drunk, but neither was they sober. And Raymond was never one to move fast at the best of times. It was like watching two slapstick comedians in slow motion.

Four of the regulars, on stools at the bar and lost in their thoughts, perked up and swivelled round to watch. One of Ebby's wild swings threw him off balance and he fell against the end one, Herbie Ozanne. Herbie tipped sideways against Tom Roussel and one by one the row of them toppled like dominoes.

Well the landlord, Wally Brouard, 18-stone and 6ft 4in, hoisted himself over the counter like an athlete and grabbed Ray and Ebby by their shirtcollars. By that time they was both breathing like asthmatics and hanging their heads. Wally turns to me and says 'Onesimus,' he says, 'take these two old fools home before I call the parish constable.' Before we knew it we was on the street walking to The Bridge, which is what the locals calls the road that goes past St Sampson's Harbour. Shaking our heads and laughing we goes into the Duke of York for a nightcap.

'What did he mean about Ebby's dad being a Quisling,' says a voice. It's young Eugene Le Patourel of the Press. He's just finished his training and was in the Flag on the lookout for scoops. He'd followed us and there he was standing by our table. He speaks to me as I was the one not fighting and was walking straighter than the others. 'You were here in the war weren't you Mr De Carteret?' He says to me.

'I was,' I nodded, 'and mon vieux, 'ow the world 'as changed since then,' I says.

Raymond and Ebby's eyes was glued to their pints. They did not fancy appearing in the paper as geriatric pugilists.

Eugene says he is writing a series called 'Occupation Jottings' or some such. And he is anxious to buy another round in exchange for my recollections. And I am happy to oblige. Ebbie and Ray nod their heads enthusiastically but still keep their lips zipped.

When we are all slurping the foam off the tops of our glasses I tell young Eugene something he did not know about me. I was an apprentice at the Press when the war started. I used to do a bit of everything, I tells him. I reported on court cases and funerals and then help set the type for the compositor.

Eugene takes his reporter's notepad out and 'is pen starts flying across the page like a demented spider. I glanced at what he was writing and saw just a load of squiggles. He explains he's using shorthand which e's spent three years learning. He reckons he can take down accurately anything said by a 'uman being, so long as it's in English. He nods encouragingly at me. Well, I don't need no encouragement., me. But he thinks my thoughts need focusing. So he asks me when the Germans first arrived in the Island.

Raymond comes back to life and says, 'June the 30th, 1940.' Then Ebby joins in and steals my thunder. 'The flower of 'itler's master race arrives at the airport,' says Ebbie, 'and starts waving shiny, new maps at the locals and wanting to know the way to Ryde...'

'We was baffled,' I chips in for, truth to tell, Ebbie wasn't there and was only repeating what he'd 'eard. He was working in his dad's vinery five miles away. I was not there either me being down at the Press helping to write a story which we headlined 'Nazis Will Give Guernsey A Miss.' But that's another story. 'We was baffled,' I says again, 'until we had a closer look at their maps of Guernsey. Cor dammy! It was the Isle of Wight. Over 20,000 troops had swallowed their own propaganda and arrived thinking they was half an hour's ferry journey from England.'

Eugene nodded at me again and rolled his eyes and looked down at his squiggles. I reckoned he was boasting when he said he could write as fast as a man can speak and was wondering how much of his hieroglyphics he would be able to read back. Eugene, a thin streak of a lad, like his father and his father's father, thought he was getting exclusive stories. But all we told him was things all us older folks knew. But every time he topped up our drinks 30 years ago seemed like yesterday.

The atmosphere got tense again when he wanted to know what a Quisling was. 'They was traitors to their own sides,' I says. 'Didn't they teach you this in history lessons at school?' I says. He says if they did he wasn't listening. I told him that some people shamed Guernsey by co-operating with the Nazis. But the rest of us decided there was nothing for it but to do what we was told. But very slow.

'Why wasn't there any resistance, like there was in France?' He asks. 'Well,' I tells him,' there wasn't much worth blowing up. Anyway, being on a small island we was all in the same boat. The Germans was pleased they wasn't on the Russian front and just wanted a quiet life.'

'Do you mean you were FRIENDLY with them?'

'We wasn't exactly friendly,' I says. 'We had our Guernsey way of getting back at them. Like when old

Xavier De Guillebon chalked "V" for Victory signs on the Germans' bike seats. When they got off they was all walking around with "V"s on their backsides. But Xavier was caught and was sent to prison for a year.'

Both Ebbie and Raymond shakes their heads mournfully at this and drains their glasses in unison like twins. I could see Eugene was getting impatient. We wasn't telling him the sort of derring-do he was thirsting for.

'Did anyone KILL any Germans?' He asks.

Raymond says there was only one German who died, and he was shot by his batman who'd gone off his head.

I says there wasn't much we could do except put up some passive resistance. There was 22,000 of them, all armed, and there was 40,000 of us with only a few airguns, catapults and garden tools. But even then they was afraid we might be whipped into rising up. So, in the end they took away our radios and censored every word in the local Press.

But they couldn't break us, I tell Eugene. We used to get up to all manner of tricks at the Press to keep our readers' spirits up. We got away with it because the Germans had no sense of humour themselves and did not understand the Guernsey mentality. We used to put all the local commandant's "Proclamations" in column five on Page One. So everyone knew it was just propaganda and to be taken with a pinch of salt. I says, 'And we used to put false messages in the public announcement columns which fooled the Nazi censor. One was from a local headmaster to the Secretary of the Education Council. It said, 'All children very fit. Tommy, Joe and Sam's boys working very hard and doing excellent work. Should graduate with honours in the near future.'

Cor we laughed.

But it was not all funny. People got deported and sent to prison in Guernsey for the slightest thing. Like Tommy Martel. He lived next door to a "Jerrybag." She gave birth to a baby fathered by a Nazi. The mother wheeled the infant's pram into the garden. 'Cor it made a bloney noise screaming and yelling. Tommy shouted over the fence in the voice of Lord Haw-Haw "Garmany calling, Garmany calling." The mother was furious and reported Tommy to the Feldpolizei and he was sent to a detention camp. We never saw him again.'

None of this excited Eugene and he starts to put his notebook away. Then he sits down again and asks what I think of today's world compared with then. 'Not much,' I says, 'Half the world is starving while the other half's got more money than they know what to do with. Criminals get luxury accommodation with regular hot meals but old people's homes are closing through lack of money.

I says when we was his age a "gay" person was the life and soul of the party, "grass" was mown, "coke" was shovelled into the boiler and "spice" was something you used to flavour food. Nothing's been the same since the war. The losers, Germany and Japan are two of the world's richest and most powerful nations. The older I get, the more I realise how little anything makes sense.

Eugene looked at us and shrugged. He picked up his notebook and put it into his pocket. We wasn't going to star in his next article.

GHOST IN THE MACHINE

Frank Broadstreet realised he'd made a serious mistake leaving the Hampton Gazette. And now their rainy day fund was gone. And there weren't enough freelance commissions to pay all the bills.

It had been the prospect of yet another year of council meetings, court coverage and cricket reports which had driven him to quit his job as Chief Reporter. But, at least he'd had a regular income. Unlike now, with his fledgling Broadstreet News Agency threatening to wither on the vine of post-Brexit recession.

Was it was only three years ago that all those contacts on the nationals and glossies had promised him plenty of work? Now they were all singing the same tune: 'Sorry, Frank old chap, we're cutting back...'

Frank sighed and booted up his Macbook Pro with full OLED keyboard (whatever that meant). He'd bought it a year ago as his reluctant gesture to modern technology, which seemed to be galloping ahead faster than his low-tech brain could cope with. He thought it would be a symbol of his new life being his own boss. And to convince himself he could flourish as a freelance he had deliberately matched the computerised miracle network now installed at his old workplace, the Gazette.

Old school reporters like him, used to hammering out copy on ancient typewriters, had become aliens in the newsrooms of today. No more cynical badinage hurled across noisy editorial offices. Now, fresh-faced graduates hunched, mesmerised, over glowing terminals - their stories re-written by the news editor even as their lovingly-crafted prose scrolled across their screens. The antiseptic silence disturbed only by the dry clacking of earnest fingers on electronic keys.

Frank shook his head. Got to move with the times, old chap, he told himself. He double-clicked on his work folder and reviewed his year's stock of stories and features as a freelance. The sparse list told its own story. His current, and last, commission was a profile on Group Captain Dick Burgess, Commanding Officer of RAF Hambourne.

The locals were continually complaining of noise and pollution from landings and takeoffs. And voices were becoming increasingly strident about the dangers of the base's ungainly transport planes overflying heavily populated communities.

Frank's profile on the Group Captain was an attempt by the county's newspaper group at balanced journalism. A chance to put the RAF's side to the populace, they said.

Frank recalled the Group Captain had seemed uncomfortable trying to explain away the near misses over the years. Frank had put it to the CO that, by the law of averages, it was only a matter of time before a tragedy occurred. Pilot error or equipment failure could mean a disastrous crash with civilian fatalities. Dick Burgess had rejected the suggestion saying it wasn't in the community's best interests to 'scaremonger.'

Frank shrugged. He'd been asked to put together an honest profile and it was all ready, bar a final check through for style. If the editor didn't like the slant, too bad.

As his eye ran idly down the list of subjects he'd tackled over the past year he frowned. There was a heading he didn't recognise. It simply said GREETINGS. He knew it wasn't one he'd written as he methodically gave every commission a date, name and number. Apart from acting as a sort of electronic filing cabinet, it was essential as a record for chasing up late payments. The word GREETINGS with no number next to it was definitely not his handiwork.

'Helen,' he shouted to his wife in the kitchen downstairs, 'have you been playing about with my computer?'

'Playing with your computer?' Her voice floated up from a distant part of the house. 'Of course not. I barely know how to switch the thing on.'

Frank looked back at the screen. The rogue file blinked at him as he manoeuvred the cursor over the word. He double-clicked. For a second the screen went blank and then a message flashed up.

'My name is Marcia. This is an experiment. Please do not be afraid. I am communicating with your writing machine from your future. I am currently in a state of hypnotic regression. Dr Malfus hypothesises that I could be under a delusion, or experiencing cryptomnesia, so I need your help. If this message is not in my dreams please reply by writing on this file some significant fact that can be verified from our encyclobank.

Frank called down the stairs. 'Helen, love, could you come to the study please.' When she arrived, not best pleased at being called away from potting up her seedlings in the utility room. Frank looked at her with mock severity. Then his face broke into a smile. 'OK Helen. So you're not a complete technophobe. Congratulations! You certainly had me fooled...but only for a second.'

Helen looked puzzled. 'Sorry, darling. I don't know what you mean.' Frank gestured at the message on the screen. The cursor was winking impatiently as if demanding a response.

Helen read the words over his shoulder. 'I thought you were supposed to be doing a profile on that Group Captain chap.' Squinting at the text, she said, 'But this certainly looks more interesting.'

'Helen, I didn't write that. You did. I just wanted to let you know I almost fell for it.'

'But, I didn't write it. Honestly. I can just about manage

our ancient laptop but I've no desire to master the intricacies of modern technology which is just so much mumbo-jumbo as far as I'm concerned.' She paused and re-read the message. 'But if I didn't write that and you obviously didn't, then who did?'

Frank realised his wife was telling the truth. And if that was the case there was only one other explanation. 'Someone must have broken into the house and for some crazy reason's left this stupid message.'

Helen shook her head. 'Surely we would have noticed it if someone had burgled the place. There are no signs and nothing's missing. And who would bother to risk being charged with breaking and entering just to leave a cryptic message which doesn't make any sense?' She pointed at the screen. 'I mean what does cryptomnesia mean? And what's an encyclobank? And who's Marcia or Dr Malfus?'

Her husband swivelled round on his chair. 'Well, how do you explain it? It couldn't be a hacker as I haven't been connected to the internet for three days now ever since the router went US.' He stroked his chin as an idea occurred. 'Unless with modern technology hackers can somehow use your electricity wiring or something. I've heard they can even use baby alarms and smart meters to get access to your computer but God knows how that works.'

'But we haven't got a baby alarm or smart meter, dear,' said Helen. Frank seemed distracted and didn't respond. 'I suppose it must be a hacker, but they usually infiltrate your system and ask for a ransom if you want to stop all your data being wiped.' He tapped a few keys and sighed with relief. 'Thank God, everything seems to be in order.'

They both peered at the words as though some clue would emerge. Eventually Helen said, 'Well, why don't you play along with it.'

Frank replied impatiently, 'I haven't got time to indulge some adolescent prankster. I've got this profile to finish. And then I've got to drum up some more work or we'll be down to selling the family silver to pay the mortgage.'

Helen's face softened. She knew how Frank was feeling. He'd tried to go it alone and fate, or Brexit and the government's bungling of the economy more like, had defeated them. Secretly she'd resigned herself to selling the house and moving into something smaller and using the capital left to bail them out.

'Look, darling,' she said, 'if neither of us can solve this mystery, just typing in a brief reply wouldn't hurt. And it might just prompt whoever's behind it to give themselves away.'

Frank looked thoughtful and then glanced at his watch. It was twenty past two. 'I've got a better idea.' He typed the words: 'Before I agree to participate in your experiment I need to satisfy myself that you are genuine. Please check your databank and give us a significant fact - for instance which horse will win this afternoon's 2.30 race at Aintree.'

Helen was watching as he typed. 'Couldn't you have come up with something a little more...well...profound?'

'Not at all. I'm showing that I can take a joke.' He chuckled. 'And if someone has hacked into this machine let's see what they come up with. You never know they might pick us a winner...'

As he was speaking Helen's eyes widened and she pointed at the screen. Frank swivelled round and watched in amazement as some phantom presence spelled out another message.

'I am pleased you regard our space-time experiment with appropriate gravitas. It is most reassuring as we have recently encountered an insurmountable difficulty in these communication experiments. In the spirit of co-operation we will answer your question. Dr Malfus has consulted our meson dimension penetrator and has established that ROMAN JESTOR will be the winner of your 2.30 race at Aintree.'

For a moment Frank was frozen in his chair. Helen continued to stare dumbly at the screen. Then Frank snapped out of his trance. 'Someone must have found a way of transmitting direct into this thing – as I said, maybe down the electricity cables themselves. Or from a transmitter nearby.' He looked relieved. 'Yes that must be it. The technology's obviously highly sophisticated...but it's still just a hoax.'

Helen replied, 'Yes, I expect you're right. But I suppose there's no harm in checking who the winner is -- '

' --Oh, come on darling. You don't actually believe that someone, or some entity from the future, can see the results of a race that hasn't happened yet.'

'No, of course not. But what harm would it do to check the result--just out of curiosity.'

Fifteen minutes later, after watching the race on television, they were back in the study peering warily at the screen. 'It's got to be a pure co-incidence,' said Frank.

'Well, I think it was amazing,' Helen said excitedly, 'ROMAN JESTOR romping home at 20-1. Think what we could have made if we'd actually backed it.'

Thirty years as a cynical journalist told Frank such miracles, not to mention world scoops, didn't happen. Especially to an old hack like him. But, perhaps the best response for now would be to pursue the electronic conversation.

Helen pulled up a chair beside his and they both stared at the winking cursor. Then Frank began to type.

'Dr Malfus's information was correct so, for the time being, we will continue. What do you wish us to do next?'

Frank had barely finished before the reply was flashing up. Whoever was at the other end was a wizard with electronics.

'I have to relay to Dr Malfus some item of information which I am unlikely to know from my own studies or knowledge. At this stage your name and location number would be the best starting point. The Doctor can then check the details in our solar history encyclobank. If I am accurate, and you do exist, then our regression experiment can proceed to the next stage - which is where previous images from our past ceased before we could confirm they were not projections from my collective unconscious.'

Helen squeezed Frank's shoulder. 'More mumbo-jumbo. But we seem to be up and running. Let's go on stringing them along. It's fun.'

More words appeared by themselves. 'As a token of his appreciation Dr Malfus says you might like to know that the winner of the 3.10 at Aintree in your present time is OH SO PRETTY.'

Frank and Helen stared at each other and then Helen broke the silence. 'Why don't we risk twenty? We can just about afford it. If we lose, it's evidence that this is just a not-so-clever hoax. But, if we win...'

Frank held up a warning hand. 'Darling, I can't believe that any of this is real. But if it is, then it seems...well...almost like getting caught up in something unnatural and dangerous.'

'All I'm saying is let's put £20 on OH SO PRETTY and see what happens. Reluctantly, Frank agreed. 'OK, I suppose it won't do any harm. I'll ring the bookies and use Mr   Visa.'

Forty minutes later Frank punched the air triumphantly. 'Four hundred quid winnings. It's incredible. I must be dreaming.' Then his smile faded. 'What am I on about? It's got to be a co-incidence. For a minute I was actually believing we had a fairy godmother from the future. But it just can't be so. It's got to be some elaborate hoax.' Helen poured her husband a large whisky and sat him down at the kitchen table.

'Let's think this all through rationally,' she said. 'If your phantom communicator is some sort of joke what's the motive? I mean if the hoaxer is after something from us what is it? In the silence that followed as Frank's brain tried to make sense of events Helen noticed the air outside the study window seemed unnaturally still. She could just detect the drone of aircraft doing circuits and bumps at the RAF base five miles away. She saw the fat outline of one of the planes sinking out of sight towards the runway.

She looked back at the screen as Frank started typing, 'Marcia, thank Dr Malfus for his information. We have won some money which we are in much need of. My wife, Helen, and I still cannot believe this is a genuine contact with our future. We will be convinced without reservation if you can tell us, accurately, the winners of the 4.15, 4.45 and 5.15 races at Chepstow this afternoon.'

'Darling, what are you doing?' Helen asked as she read the words.

'Sweetheart, if this isn't some kind of prank we might as well make use of it. We don't know how long this contact will last. I mean they might have a cosmic storm or Marcia might lose her concentration or a thousand other whims of a capricious fate could sever communications.

'If I get these tips from Malfus I'm going to put our £400 winnings on a treble.'

Helen looked doubtful, then her face cleared, 'I suppose we haven't got much to lose. And all this,' she gestured at the blinking oblong of light on the screen, 'is so fantastic we might actually pull it off.'

As she was speaking a reply began spelling itself out on the screen. 'Dr Malfus is much amused at the concept of money. Here, in our dimension, we do not need such crude barter systems. However, the names you want are APPOLLO, TIME OUT and INDIAN TONIC respectively.'

'Well,' said Helen consulting the race card in her Daily Telegraph, 'they're all listed as running. Let's go for it.' As she spoke, the windows rattled and the desk shook as another military transport aircraft flew low over the house. Frank looked out of the study window to see the four-engined leviathan rumble over the hill to line up for landing.

He made a mental note to adjust his profile on the

Group Captain. They must have changed their flight paths recently, because the house seemed to be right under it today. And he had just witnessed, first hand, an example of low flying over civilian property which the CO had denied.

But for now he had more immediate matters on his mind.

Later that same evening a stunned Frank and Helen Broadstreet were half-way through a vintage bottle of Champagne. They'd had it for months waiting for something suitable to celebrate. But events of the afternoon had eclipsed their wildest imaginings.

'How much did you say we've won?' Helen asked Frank for the third time.

Reluctantly, Frank dragged his mind from its reverie. 'Darling, I keep telling you. Plus or minus a few thousand I make it half a million.'

'Frank, my darling, I've never, ever experienced such an amazing day. Just think what we can do with that kind of money. We can pay off the mortgage, go on a luxury holiday, buy a new car...'

She added thoughtfully, 'We could even move. I do love our little house but I hate those planes droning overhead day and night. We could find somewhere quieter, with a fitted kitchen and a fully-equipped, hi-tech study. And you can get down to writing that book you've always talked about in wonderful peace and quiet...'

Frank smiled. It gave him a warm feeling to see her so happy. Life married to a journalist hadn't been much fun. He'd had to work all hours, and when he came home he'd be tired and scratchy. He'd really relish making her happy now and giving her everything she'd always wanted.

And he owed it all to...who? There had to be a rational explanation. They weren't really in contact with beings 200 years in the future were they? It was beyond belief. And yet...Every horse had come up and they were sitting on a fortune.

He'd checked with the bookies after the last race and they'd assured him, albeit with a trace of reluctance, his winnings would be paid direct to his Visa card. Everything looked pretty watertight. What could possibly go wrong?

'Darling Helen, I think we should thank Marcia,' he said.

'Let's go up and tell her the good news. We can say we definitely accept she's genuine and the least we can do is co-operate with their experiment.' The thought occurred to Frank that, besides his new-found wealth, he'd be famous the world over if all this turned out to be genuine and scientifically verifiable.

As they walked through the study door they both saw another message on the screen. It read, 'Despite earlier promising signs we are sad to tell you we have encountered the same insurmountable flaw with this experiment as with the others. Contact will be broken off when you cease later.'

Frank and Helen looked at each other. 'What do they mean, when you cease later? It's not us ceasing with the contact it's them. For whatever reason, they're pulling out. It's all getting a bit suspicious. It sounds like the jokers are getting cold feet.'

'Just to satisfy my curiosity, darling, ask Marcia what she means,' said Helen.

The house rattled again as another plane rumbled overhead. Frank began tapping the keyboard. 'What insurmountable flaw? And what do you mean by...when we cease later? When we cease contact, perhaps?' And he added with a final flourish, 'You can come clean now. Is all this some kind of elaborate hoax?'

The reply unfolded on the screen. 'We fear there might be an immutable universal law that permits us contact only with those who cannot endanger the future by passing on their knowledge. We have concluded this because, so far, all the entities we have conversed with have ceased.

'Until now we had believed these contacts were imaginary, and in my collective unconscious only. You are the first we have been able to confirm through our encyclobank as having existed. But you will cease later, too.'

Frank was baffled, 'Darling what do you make of this? Why does Marcia keep talking about us ceasing..?'

As they reflected on the riddle he was conscious of the sound of another aircraft engine. This time, though, there was something different about it.

He hunched over the terminal and rattled off another question, 'Marcia, please explain what you mean by the word "cease"?'

A sentence silently unfolded in reply, 'Forgive us. We forget that we no longer understand the concept of life and death. Here we are continuous beings. You will understand the word "cease" better as "die."'

'Oh, my God,' gasped Helen. 'She says we're going to die.'

As husband and wife stared in horror at the screen, their attention shifted to the window. They watched in disbelief as the outline of a massive, burning aircraft fusilage and wings hurtled towards them. A shattering roar of aircraft engines filled the house as a fireball of metal and brick merged and fused in one cataclysmic eruption.

Frank and Helen Broadstreet felt no pain as they ceased to exist. They never read the last words appearing on the screen as the house was vapourised. 'You asked if this is all a   hoax.   The   truth   is…'

HA-HA YOU'RE DEAD

A bad case of piles was the worst a lifetime of postings to the hotspots of the world had bequeathed Colonel Algernon Cuthbert Fairfax OBE, CBE (Military).

So it was ironic that, although he didn't know it, he was now surrounded by enemies. And that retirement to the pastoral delights of the Sussex countryside would be the death of him.

As he got out of bed and stepped towards his en suite bathroom, a glance across the lawn, over the ha-ha and on to the fields and downs beyond, froze him in mid-stride.

'What the bloody Hell,' the Colonel thundered as he flung open his upstairs bedroom window. His fury had little effect on the trespassing heifers ruminating placidly amidst the artistry of his beloved garden.

His blood pressure surged to seizure level as he took in

the devastation. The pond was polluted, his prize dahlias flattened and the ornamental lawn a travesty of yesterday's velvety, manicured perfection.

The Colonel's neighbours on both sides paused as the decibels rattled their breakfast crockery. 'Poor Colonel Fairfax,' clucked Theodora Twitchett as she spread another dollop of home-made crab-apple jam onto the Victoria sponge she was making.

Miss Twitchett, whose love of animals was equalled only by her antipathy to most members of the human race, exchanged looks with her dachshund Barnaby and licked the last of the preserve from her fingers with a flourish. 'I'd say the day's got off to a most promising start, wouldn't you Barney my precious,' she said.

In the kitchen of the cottage on the other side of the Fairfaxs' Tudor residence, Bert Golightly caught his wife's eye. Pamela Golightly assumed the casual expression she'd been obliged to practice a lot recently.

'I wonder what's upset our Algie?' said Bert with a note of grim satisfaction in his voice. Inwardly, he smiled a secret smile. Whatever it was, the treacherous swine had a lot worse coming to him yet.

Meanwhile, next door Patience Fairfax held half-heartedly onto the belt of her husband's dressing gown as he leaned precariously outwards. She resisted the temptation to let go. Seeing him fall into the rhododendrons would not have been adequate compensation for what she'd suffered over the years. She had more ambitions plans for retribution.

'Careful, darling. Remember what the doctor said about your blood pressure.'

Reluctantly, the Colonel subsided allowing himself to be tugged back to a less perilous angle. His face, permanently florid from too many ports at too many Regimental dinners, was an additional shade of apoplectic purple. 'Bugger my blood pressure,' he rasped. 'What's that herd of bovine Barbarians doing in my garden?'

The Hon Mrs Patience Fairfax followed the Colonel's pointing finger, which was trembling with indignation. She saw that, having devoured everything within grazing height, the intruders were now returning in single file back to their field.

'Who the Hell unbolted that gate?' Demanded her husband, tugging furiously at his dressing gown cord which had now knotted itself at the sash. He snarled, 'Two years of meticulous nurturing ruined. Had me eye on Chelsea next year. That's gone for a Burton. Someone's going to pay dearly for this...'

About 50 feet from where the Colonel was breathing vengeance Miss Twitchett sat Barnaby on her lap and tickled him behind his ears. 'Now I wonder what it is the Colonel's so upset about,' she asked rhetorically.' As if we didn't know.' Barnaby winced as his mistress stroked his back soothingly. He still hadn't fully recovered from the effects of that vicious kick.

As Miss Twitchett hummed to herself, Bert Golightly had emerged from his kitchen, whose door led to the garden which adjoined the Fairfaxs. He peered at next door's scene of devastation from behind his Dorothy Wheatcroft floribunda rosebush.

He took in the churned-up lawn, pock-marked borders and drunkenly-swaying pergolas.

Suddenly, a parade-ground command cut through the

air. 'Golightly, stay right where you are.' Through the rose-stems Bert saw Colonel Fairfax bearing down on him. He was wielding a double-barrelled shotgun.

'Er, I think I may have a touch of sooty mould,' said Bert nervously eyeing the gun.

'Damn your sooty mould,' harrumphed the Colonel. 'D'yer know anything about this...this...abomination?' He waved at the source of his anger. 'I always keep that gate bolted. Someone deliberately undid it and let those blasted beasts in.'

Before Bert could reply Miss Twitchett's refined tones drifted from her side of the garden. 'I see you've had a visitation, Colonel,' She was on tiptoes, peering over the fence. 'What a terrible mess...Your lovely borders and your beautiful lawn. I was only saying to Barney the other day, it would do justice to a bowling green...'

'Barney? Who's...er...Oh, quite so.' The Colonel recalled catching the bloody animal a week or so ago burrowing in his border. A hefty boot up the nether regions had sent it squealing back to its own territory.

'Years of work down the drain,' Miss Twitchett. 'Any idea who might have left the gate open..?'

'I'm afraid I can't imagine,' said Miss Twitchett. Then her face took on a thoughtful expression. 'Unless it was something to do with those strange voices I heard in the early hours. Barney must have heard them too because he started growling - '

' - Strange voices? What strange voices?' The Colonel's eyebrows descended and writhed like two angry caterpillars.

'It just sounded like a couple of youngsters from the village on their way home. So I didn't think anything of it at the time. I assumed they were a little the worse for drink. But I must admit I was puzzled when they seemed to stop and hold a whispered conversation.'

The Colonel's nostrils flared as he got the scent of his quarry. 'Go on, Miss Twitchett. What were these whisperers saying?'

'Of course, Colonel, I couldn't be sure but I think I heard one mentioning something about "revenge" and another said they'd be back tonight to...er... "finish it..."'

Her neighbour's complexion began turning the colour of an aubergine. 'Revenge, Eh? We'll see about that. I've served Queen and country and fought the dregs of the world for 40 years. Any young tearaway who tries to get the better of me is going to get a nasty shock.'

As if to emphasise his point he brandished the shotgun still clutched in a practised fist.

'If these young bounders show up tonight they'll get both barrels up their backsides.'

Bert returned to the cottage. This needed thinking about. When he'd decided to make Fairfax pay dearly for what he'd done, he'd fantasised shooting him. Or stabbing him to death and feeding him piece by piece into the garden shredder. As he'd dwelt on his neighbour's wrongdoing, Bert's mind had taken off into even more lurid flights of fancy. He'd drug the old codger and drive him to an abandoned cottage in the woods. There, he'd tie him, naked, to the bed and make him beg for mercy. Then he'd use his pruning shears to exact justice.

But in the end Bert had admitted to himself that he just wasn't the sort to wreak such violence. So, he'd conceived a diabolical plan to make the Colonel suffer a slow, drawn-out mental and emotional agony. It was simplicity itself. Every now and again, over the weeks, Bert would wait until dark. Then he'd nip next door and spray the petrol he kept for the lawnmower, over selected areas of Fairfax's hallowed turf. Its velvety smoothness just asked to be desecrated.

The petrol would be invisible, but after a few days scattered brown patches would appear. Whatever remedial action the Colonel took would be to no avail. Fairfax loved that lawn so much his torment and frustration would be unbearable. And, Bert mused, he could watch Fairfax suffer as he'd been made to suffer. Unfortunately, though, vandals - if that old bag of bones Miss Twitchett was to be believed - had got there first.

Late that night Algernon Fairfax sat under the pear tree at the edge of the ha-ha's retaining wall. He could hear the trickle of water into the pond three feet below. There was no moon and clouds had blotted out the stars. His shotgun was in his lap. A blanket across his knees, and frequent nips from a hip-flask of Cognac, kept out the cold.

In reflecting on the motives of the hooligans responsible for the desecration he'd come to the conclusion they must have been a couple of the ne'er-do-wells he dealt with on a weekly basis as chairman of the local magistrates. He'd said it before and he'd say it again, they should bring back conscription. Putting some of these tearaways in the hands of a sarn't-major would soon sort 'em out.

His ears strained to hear any unusual sounds. He'd made up his mind. If he caught the blighters in the act he'd march them at the point of his gun back to the house and dial 999.

With every swig of brandy he became increasingly confident that before dawn the culprits would be explaining themselves to the law. He could then get the landscape gardeners in and the blasted vandals would be ordered to foot the bill. Revenge? He'd show 'em revenge.

Just then, he heard a noise. A sort of scraping and whispering. It seemed to be coming from the direction of Miss Twitchett's garden. He fumbled for the flashlight and got unsteadily to his feet.

As he stepped forward something became entangled with his legs. The brandy which had given him comfort from the creeping cold was befuddling his brain. Swaying, he screwed up his eyes and peered into the darkness

As he struggled to keep his balance a shape loomed in front of him. His feet were firmly caught and he felt himself beginning to topple. Something that seemed like a pair of hands pushed at his chest and he lurched backwards over the edge of the wall into the pond. There was a splash and both barrels of the shotgun roared into the night.

'He died instantly', said the doctor to the Colonel's wife, after the neighbours, muttering their condolences, had returned home. 'Somehow the blanket got wrapped round his feet and he fell into the pond. The gun went off and, well, it seems it was a tragic accident. I'm so sorry...'

After the doctor, and the ambulance, had gone Patience Fairfax poured herself a fortifying whisky. She hadn't meant it to turn out like this. When she'd let those cows in last night to trample his beloved garden it was just her pathetic attempt at retribution for all his affairs over the years. His latest, with Pam Golightly next door, had been the last straw. Poor Bert. He obviously hadn't suspected. But now he'd need never know.

She took another sip of her drink. She was puzzled. If she had let the cattle in through the gate, it followed that there couldn't have been any vandals. And, if there hadn't been any vandals, why had Miss Twitchett said she'd heard strange voices plotting revenge? She shrugged. What did it matter? It was all working out for the best. Her husband's insurances would leave her comfortably off and there'd be no more humiliations.

Next door, a stunned Pam Golightly had finally gone back to bed. Bert thought that she'd disguised the shock of her lover's untimely end with an award-winning performance. Now, he'd never have to confront her with her...her...fling. A feeling of elation coursed through him.

In a sense he'd committed the perfect murder. He'd contemplated all kinds of vengeance and now the Colonel was dead. But it was really thanks to tearaways from the village, according to the dog woman. Funny that, thought Bert. He hadn't heard a thing last night and he was usually wide awake at the first sound of an odd noise. He supposed it was old Twitchett's dachshund that had alerted her.

It was strange how fate worked things out, he thought. If

hooligans hadn't let those cows into Fairfax's garden, the old fool wouldn't have been waiting in ambush - then become drunk and incapable obligingly falling into the pond and shooting himself. Justice had been done, Bert decided.

As the first blackbird began the dawn chorus, Miss Twitchett was going over events with Barnaby. 'When we saw Mrs Fairfax opening that gate we knew exactly how to get our revenge, didn't we my pet?' Barnaby gazed up lovingly at his mistress, who seemed particularly pleased with herself this morning.

She went on, 'Make up a little story about hooligans from the village. And drop a hint that they'd be back that night and we knew he couldn't resist lying in wait.'

She gave Barney half a digestive biscuit. 'That's for being a clever boy and tripping him up.' She popped the other half into her mouth. 'And the rest's for me for pushing him into the pond.'

Nobody, she thought, kicked her dog and got away with it.

DOGON

I saw the myth called Dogon

Standing in the sky,

He asked me what I wanted

And wept at my reply.

He called up black-eyed shadows

To rail and writhe and rave,

They took the path to Glory

But ended in the grave.

I shook my head at Dogon

He turned his face away,

My banquet was of riches

Exchanged for a soul one day.

Too late! The infernal madness

Snuffed out the fractured light,

I became a dark-eyed Shadowy One

Adding to the night.

Dogon grieved, then moved away

Another soul to find,

He came upon an infant

Deaf and mute and blind

Who smiled at him in pleasure

Needing nothing more,

This is the truth, said Dogon

Tell it to the poor.

GOODNIGHT BELOVED DADDY

The old man's eyes were closed and saliva trickled from the corner of his mouth to a damp patch on the pillow. His bony hands gripped the edge of the sheet as if to keep the world from seeing his shame. His eyelids fluttered as he dreamed of his beautiful Gracie. It was the end of his worst day yet. Only sleep had brought him peace. All three of them, standing now around his bed, wished for all their sakes that he was dead.

She couldn't carry on any longer, Catherine Dickenson told herself. She couldn't bear to see the father she loved so tormented. It was as if he was possessed by a malevolent spirit. In two years it had turned him from a strong man with a quiet dignity into a raving, frothing imposter. She'd made up her mind: tonight she was going to put an end to it.

The doctors had said there was nothing they could do; just

tranquillisers for the day and a sedative at night. They'd reluctantly confided there was no other answer to this kind of dementia. They'd called it by its clinical name - Alzheimer's Disease.

But, thought Catherine, their prognosis hadn't prepared her for what her family had gone through. Every day had brought new horrors. As he'd deteriorated, her beloved daddy had turned into an incontinent shouting, clapping, weeping monster.

After today's new madness she'd made up her mind...It wouldn't be murder. You couldn't murder someone you loved, could you?

No, murder was for drugs cartels, gangland feuds, thugs. It would be - what did the newspapers call it? A Mercy Killing? Yes, it would be like ending the suffering of an animal. It was her duty. She'd just give him enough of his sleeping pills to ensure a gentle, merciful release. She wouldn't tell anyone; it would be her secret. And she'd do it tonight.

Catherine was startled out of her reverie as her daughter's hand slipped into hers. 'Don't look so sad mummy. He's alright now. He was just having one of his turns. Come downstairs and I'll make us a nice cup of tea.'

Catherine squeezed Jane's fingers. 'In a minute. Stay with me - just while I collect my thoughts. 'She looked across the bed at her husband, Edward, who was standing, staring down at the mound under the blankets with such hatred in his eyes. What had this nightmare done to them all? She wondered.

The piercing, animal wail that had brought the three of them running to Thomas Middleton's bedroom was now part of a daily Hell they all shared.

Edward Dickenson clenched his fists until they hurt. He'd like to smash the figure on the bed and stop its antics forever. 'Why don't you just die,' he muttered under his breath.

As it always did these days, his anger changed to helplessness. He'd chased every quack remedy and failed. He'd begged Catherine to put the old man into a home but she wouldn't hear of it. He looked at his hands. They were trembling.

It hadn't always been like this, Edward admitted to himself. Tom had been a good-natured and supportive father-in-law. But as soon as his beloved wife, Grace, had died of cancer the rot had set in. Tom's spark had gone and he'd become remote. He'd reluctantly agreed to sell up and move in with them. After that they began to notice little aberrations; forgetful moments.

'What's for supper tonight?' He'd ask Catherine, rubbing his hands in that way of his.

'Your favourite - cod steaks in parsley sauce,' she'd reply. Thirty seconds later he'd rub his hands in anticipation and ask, 'What's for supper tonight?'

At first they'd all laughed it off.

'Anno domini gets us all in the end,' Edward would joke, rubbing his hand over the few scraps of hair that still clung to his head. And they'd all smile. But they weren't smiling now. Not at the wrong end of 18 hours of nursing that poor, pathetic vegetable. Not after 18 months of watching Tom Middleton turn into an unrecognisable bag of bones.

Edward felt so impotent. If only there was something he could do. His eyes strayed to Tom's bottle of sleeping tablets on the bedside table. Just a few of those would stop the torment for all of them. His father-in-law would be put out of his misery and Catherine's nightmare would be over.

'Come off it, you old fool,' he said to himself, 'you're too weak. Don't kid yourself that you've got the guts to carry out a murder. Yes, murder. That's what it'd be.'

He bit his lip. But, he couldn't stand the thought of watching his wife fall apart. Every day a little bit more of her died. And every day he hated himself for his impotence.

He unclenched his fists and looked across the bed at his wife and daughter. 'Let's go downstairs and enjoy what little peace we can while it lasts,' he sighed.

Jane Dickenson watched her father go through the door. Poor daddy. He so wanted to solve this family crisis but there was nothing left he could do. She squeezed her mother's arm a little tighter. If only there was something...Jane thought.

She hated to admit it but grandad would be better off

dead. He must suffer agonies of remorse and shame in his odd lucid moments. The alien he'd now become was so destructive. It was heartbreaking to see what it was doing to poor mummy. She looked more like 65 than 45.And dad's roly-poly good humour was a rare commodity these days.

Jane looked at the figure on the bed, sleeping so peacefully now. Then she noticed the round, plastic bottle next to the clock on the bedside table. Just a few of those pills would solve all of their problems.

She started. It was funny, they'd debated the whole issue of mercy killing at college. 'This house believes euthanasia to be a prerequisite of a civilized society...' Jane recalled she had proposed the motion and it had been upheld by an overwhelming majority...

Standing next to Jane, lost in her own thoughts, Catherine looked down on the man who's life she was going to end.

I love you, father, she thought. But I can't watch you suffer any longer. I'm not strong enough, you see.

Suddenly he opened his eyes, as if he'd read her mind.

But he was looking beyond her - into his own, secret world. At moments like this he seemed almost...content.

You'll soon be happy for ever, daddy. Forgive me, she implored silently.

A little later downstairs, Edward put mugs of tea in front of his wife and daughter and slid into his chair at the kitchen table. He looked at Catherine's drawn, defeated face.

He said resolutely, 'He's got to go.'

Jane took her mother's hand. 'Daddy, don't. Mum's had enough to cope with today.'

'Jane, don't stop me now. I've been meaning to say this for months.' He looked into his wife's eyes. There was a terrible sadness there. He went on gently, 'The old chap's impossible now, uncontrollable. He must go into a home.' He held up his hand to forestall Catherine's objections. 'It's not fair on any of us but especially you...' He added brutally, 'Look at you, you're worn out. You're old before your time. What sort of life have you got now? You're full-time nurse to an incontinent vegetable.'

Catherine pushed her mug away. 'I can't do it to him. I can't leave him to strangers.'

Jane said, 'I hate the thought, too, mummy. But I agree with daddy. It can't be right for us as a family to go on suffering this...this...relentless wretchedness. You've done your best. No-one could have done more...It's now time for you to be strong enough to let him go...Be strong for us.'

Edward broke the silence that followed. 'There is another way.' He looked at both women avoiding their eyes.

'What other way, daddy?'

Edward hesitated and then plunged on, 'The poor old chap could be put out of his misery.' The two women looked at him in bewilderment. Eventually Catherine said, 'You surely don't mean...what I think you mean..?'

Edward nodded. 'It would be a merciful release.'

'What, kill him. Murder my own father..?'

Edward shifted uncomfortably. 'I don't like that word. What I mean is...is...to ease dad out of this. It would be so easy and painless to release him from it. All we'd have to do is give him a few more sleeping tablets than his normal dose and let him drift away...'

Catherine slammed both hands down on the kitchen table shaking her head. 'I don't believe I'm hearing this. How could either of you imagine I could do that to my own father? I could never live with myself. And, we'd all be accessories to murder. The idea's unthinkable. I'm going to forget we had this conversation.'

Angrily, she collected up the mugs and put them in the sink ready for washing in the morning. 'And now I'm going to bed - it'll probably be another long day tomorrow.' As she closed the door behind her, she hoped she'd been convincing. They mustn't suspect what she was planning. The act of ending her father's life would be hers and hers alone.

In the darkened room upstairs, Thomas Middleton's eyes fluttered open. For a moment he couldn't think where he was and he reached under the bedclothes to touch his wife, sleeping by his side, for reassurance. She wasn't there. And then he remembered. Grace had died. They'd been part of each other's lives for 46 years.

Their first meeting was as vivid to him as if it was happening now in this very room. She'd got into the same train as him and he couldn't take his eyes off her all the way to Brighton. Later he'd called her his "MBEB" - my blue eyed beauty. How they'd laughed. And, over the years, laughter had filled their lives.

They'd been so happy. A perfect couple, people said. And when little Cath had been born, it had made their family complete. Good times.

He patted the empty space where Grace had lain all those years. Yes, good times, my darling. Where are you now, Eh? Are you waiting for me? How I long to talk to you again. Hear your lovely voice. See that smile.

I'm useless to anyone now, you know. My mind's going. Don't shake your pretty head and give me your exasperated look. It's true. I don't know where I am. There are strangers all round me. There's no-one who cares about me any more. Not like you cared.

Do you know, I dream of you every day. And those dreams are so real. All the colours are so bright and I'm overwhelmed by your love.

I want to sleep for ever, to be with you for ever, my dearest Gracie. When I'm awake, you're like a ghost in my imaginings. But, it's not enough. I want to touch you, Gracie. I want to feel your arms round me. I feel safe with you...His thoughts were interrupted by the creak of a stair. He whispered, 'Shhh!, I can hear someone coming. It's probably one of those strangers I told you about...'

Catherine slipped quietly into the room. 'Daddy, who were you talking to? I know you're awake.'

'Who're you.'

'I'm Catherine, daddy, your daughter. It's time for you to take your pill.'

'You're not my daughter, my daughter's little Cath...And I don't want any pills. What're they for?'

'You always take one, every night,' Catherine coaxed. 'They're to give you a good sleep. Come on, sit up. I've brought you some warm milk to help it go down.'

Catherine unscrewed the top of the bottle. Now was the moment. Just feed them one by one into her father's mouth until they were all gone. No-one would ever know.

He would pass peacefully away. If any questions were asked she'd just say he must have woken up in the night and taken them all in his confusion. A tragic mistake.

As she supported the back of his head to help him sit up he gripped her left wrist with both hands.

'Gracie, there you are. I've been waiting for you. Take me away from here. Take me home...'

Catherine couldn't stop the tears as she saw the desperation in his face. Then his eyes - suddenly those of the father she used to know - looked into hers. Her heart wrung with pity as he said, 'What's happening to me Cath..?' The question hung in the silence between them. His agony tore at her soul and she knew she couldn't do it. She put the capsules back on the bedside table.

'We'll forget the sleeping pill tonight father. I think you're probably tired enough. I'll leave you the milk in case you get thirsty.' She lowered him onto the pillow and kissed his forehead.

'Sweet dreams.' She put the light out and left the door slightly ajar.

An hour later Thomas Middleton was still awake.

He whispered into the darkness, 'Gracie, are you there my darling?' He imagined he could see his wife, like a wraith, at the bottom of the bed. But he couldn't make out the shape. Why was it she only seemed real in his dreams? He was suddenly struck by an idea. Why hadn't he thought of it before? He could make dreams couldn't he? They came from those little pills. They were his key to reality. His doorway to happiness. Gracie would be there, as she always was, waiting for him...

He groped for the bottle and with feverish strength unscrewed the lid and poured the capsules into his trembling mouth. The wraith seemed to be at his side now, supporting his cupped hands, as he drank deeply of the still warm milk. 'That's right, Gracie, help me. It won't be long now and we'll be together, like always.'

He lay back on the pillow. 'There My Blue Eyed Beauty. There. Just a little while now and we'll be together for ever...'

Then the shadows in the room seemed to deepen as if a door had closed.

WE'RE ONLY HUMAN, AFTER ALL'S SAID AND DONE

Buffo Gloucester Old-Spots squinted down the telescopic sight until the cross-hairs sprang into focus. This was going to be an easy kill. Despite its age, the 21st-century Tasco laser sight was still the best in the business. It placed the red dot just above the man's heart. Him first, his mate next. Buffo squeezed the trigger gently.

He and Clarence had been tracking the pair for the last six hours. Now, they had nowhere further to run. The man, and his female companion, were plainly exhausted. Buffo saw the magnified images hold hands as they slid down the cul-de-sac wall.

It was only four in the afternoon but already the light was beginning to fade behind the industrial haze that permanently shrouded the sun these days. Buffo glanced sideways at his 36th - or was it his 37th - son? Instead of the bloodlust which should have been shining from the three-year-old's piggy eyes, Clarence's expression was a mixture of pity and puzzlement.

Buffo hesitated. He had to shoot now or his target might yet find a second wind and disappear into the shadows of the crumbling city. 'What's the matter, son? You know we've got to do it.'

Clarence Gloucester Old-Spots looked pleadingly back at his father, his snout twitching with emotion. 'But why, dad? What harm have they done us?'

His father grunted kindly. 'It's not a question of harm, son. It's the law. Any sub-pig found outside its reservation must be shot on sight.'

Clarence snorted, 'I think it's a stupid law. Look at them, dad. All they were doing was scavenging in their old habitat. Why have we got to kill them? It seems so...so...pointless.'

Buffo replied firmly, 'I'm sorry son but the law's the law. If we let these sub-pigs go who knows what harm they might do to our world. That's the whole point of the culling programme. We have to keep their numbers within manageable bounds and under our control. That's why we gave them reservations to live on.'

Buffo turned and swung the old hunting rifle up to his

shoulder again. The sub-pigs were still there. Beasts resigned to their fate. Deep down inside, some atavistic sense of compassion nagged at him. Why couldn't they have made a run for it while his attention had lapsed? He thought.

The plaintive voice of his boy broke into Buffo's thoughts again. 'Why do they do it, dad? Why don't these humans just stay in their reservations and enjoy their lives? Why are they always escaping back to these old ruins?'

Buffo winced and looked around furtively. He hissed, 'Don't EVER use that H-word. If anyone reported you we could both end up at the abattoir.' He intoned sternly, 'At all times they're to be called sub-pigs and, as such, they have no rights.'

'Sorry dad,' Clarence whispered. 'But why do we have to kill them?' His face crinkled, perplexed. 'In fact why can't pigs and hum...er...sub-pigs live together?'

Buffo sighed and shook his head in wonderment at his son's naivety. He put a trotter round Clarence's shoulder and pulled him closer. How could he explain it in simple terms? Despite the benefit of his human brain cells poor little Clarence was pig-ignorant. He must be a throwback, thought Buffo.

He explained gently, 'It's like this, son. Three hundred years ago, back in the 1990's, animals called homo sapiens ran everything. They were an arrogant species and in the end hubris came with a terrible swiftness. They were struck down in their millions by a disease they could find no cure for...'

'...like swine-fever, dad?'

Buffo smiled indulgently. 'Yes, son, like swine-fever. It swept the globe and decimated their race. They might even have survived that, though. But the plague happened to co-incide with their genetic experiments on us pigs.'

'What sort of experiments, dad?'

'Well, they wanted to cure people with bad hearts, or livers, by transplanting ours into their hum...ah...sub-pig bodies. As you can imagine, it might have seemed a good idea for them but it wasn't too healthy for us. This was typical of their attitude, though. Self, self, self... Anyway, I digress.

'Our hearts were having none of it. They rejected their human hosts and it was back to the drawing board. Until, that is, scientists started injecting us with their sub-pig genes. Straight away our hearts started to co-operate and suddenly we were being turned out in our thousands just to supply people with spare parts.'

'Sounds like a brilliant idea, dad.'

Buffo looked into his son's innocent, wrinkled face and groaned under his breath. Clarence was as thick as pig-muck. 'Look, son, it was just another example of their arrogance. Once again, they were tampering with nature. They'd been at it since homo erectus in the Palaeolithic era. By the time they reached the end of the 20th century they'd become homo sapiens and had nigh-on ruined the world.'

'It's hard to believe, dad, that these funny, spindly things could ever have run anything. So what happened next?'

'Ah, well, that's where the revenge of the gods came in.' Clarence looked puzzled again and Buffo hurried on, 'They'd flown in the face of nature too long. It was what you might call a classic example of an ill-wind. Because in mixing their genes with ours...' Buffo allowed himself a grunt of satisfaction '...homo sapiens got just a bit too clever for their own good and it backfired on them. And the world was never the same again.'

Clarence scratched his head and blinked his piggy eyes. 'I don't understand, dad. What backfired?'

Buffo shot a quick glance through the gathering gloom. He could just make out two immobile shapes, still slumped against the crumbling wall. He looked down at Clarence's earnest features. 'What they didn't reckon on was their hum...er...sub-pig...genes went straight to our heads and mingled with our brain cells. The result: we became more intelligent than them.

'And put that brainpower in these tough old bodies of ours and the boot was rapidly on the other trotter, so to speak. While mankind was laid waste with disease, we organised ourselves and took over.'

'And now we're the top dogs..?'

'...er...yes, son.'

Clarence's floppy ears flapped over his eyes as he shook his head in bewilderment. 'But I still don't see why we have to hunt them down. Why can't we leave them alone?'

Buffo cradled his head in his trotters and massaged his tired eyes. He was beginning to wish he'd stayed with the drove and not opted to take his half-wit offspring on this expedition. He took a deep breath and patted Clarence's leg. 'Look, son,' he said patiently, 'what you see against that wall over there was once the most dangerous animal on earth. And it could be again...

'If we don't keep it strictly under control it'll run riot again. You see by the end of the 20th century man's pollution had filled the skies, rivers and seas with plastic and poison. They'd cut down the rainforests, grubbed out ancient woodlands, torn up the countryside with motorways, hunted the whale almost to extinction...' A surge of poetic creativity added a fiery passion to Buffo's final words '...And the flora and fauna of Spaceship Earth found itself staring into the abyss.'

After a brief silence, which hung heavily in the false twilight, Clarence said uncertainly, 'But the air and the rivers and the seas are still poisoned. We cut all the rest of the rainforests down ourselves and there are no ancient woodlands left to grub up. And all the motorways are clogged with our pigmobiles, factories belch out smoke day and night and the countryside is one big swamp. And...and...what's a whale, dad..?'

Buffo cleared his throat and grunted awkwardly, 'You're too young to understand, son. We had a new world to build. We couldn't let sentimentality stand in our way.'

Clarence remembered something he'd been watching in his Virtual Reality history lesson the day before. 'But the sub-pigs couldn't have been that bad. They had lots of people who cared, like Friends of the Earth and Greenpeace and the World Wide Fund for Nature. They were always fighting to keep an ecological balance in the world.'

With childish logic he nodded his head eagerly. 'And they still had birds and mammals and butterflies and wild flowers. Now, the only ones left are those in the hum...um...sub-pig reservations.'

Then Clarence was struck by a brilliant thought. 'Why don't we copy Homo Sapiens and make Nature Conservation Areas full of creatures and plants like...like...lots of wildlife parks. The animals would breed and we could fill the Earth with beauty again, dad.'

Buffo shook his head sadly. The lad was obviously a few sties short of a piggery. Buffo said reflectively, 'An Earth full of beauty might have suited your common or garden Porker. But it's no use to us.' He lowered his voice to a whisper. 'You must understand, Clarence my son. It's not in our nature. Don't forget, we might be pigs on the outside but inside we're only human.'

With that, Buffo raised his gun for the last time. He flicked on the infra-red image-intensifier and pulled the trigger twice. The two shadowy forms jerked and fell sideways. They were still holding hands.

EATING OUT WITH THE GLITTERATI

I'm here, my man, I've parked the Rolls, can't wait to eat and be seen

My usual spot by the fireplace, please, the one reserved for the Queen,

What do you mean, who am I? Where's the maitre d'?

He's down with salmonella, Ma'am, you'll have to make do with me.

I'm famous, you see, so let's agree (your squeaky shoes or no)

That when I flick my fingers, I want my importance to show.

There I was, my Lady, retired three years and a day

When the owner rang and begged me (he said he'd double my pay!)

Your financial arrangements are of no account, to one of the glitterati

I wrote a literary novel, you know, and now I'm a VIP

So sorry, my Lady, but as you can see, there's not a place to spare

Your friends got here before you and are disinclined to share.

Come, come, Dear Charles (can I call you Charles?) just find me a corner seat

And I'll say no more about it – and I don't even need to eat;

I'm ever so sorry, your Ladyship, but I've asked around the floor

Rich and famous they may be, but their charity rating's poor.

I can't believe it, Charlie, I know them every one

There's Tania B and Joany C and the Earl of whatsisname's son.

There there, my Lady, they're all for show, and shallow as the ebbin' tide

Lord L's a fraud, so's Lady D and the Colonel's much more beside.

Now they're laughing at me, I feel so low, cannot you just pretend

To be showing me to a private room, for a chat with a

famous friend?

I can't, my Lady, but come this way, there's a message you must heed

There's someone who'd like to meet you and say thank you for your good deed.

I'm sorry Chas it can't be me, for others I've cared not a jot

I haven't assisted a soul, a friend in need or not

Ah my dear, but you did, a long time ago to be sure

A beggar asked for a fiver and you gave him five times more

Now you mention it, I do remember, but I did it just to impress

The rich friends who accompanied me, to show off my largesse.

But it wasn't the money, My Lady, that carried the day just then

The kind words you whispered to him, made him the greatest of men.

He invested the money you gave him and took your words to his heart

And over the years his empire has more than played its part

In helping those like he was, with no hope of a future life,

Who went on to spread compassion and prevent much war and strife.

But Charles who is this Saint, who I can only just recall?

Why he's standing before you Ma'am, but Saint I'm not at all

Just an ordinary man in the gutter who received an angel's touch

And was inspired to give his life - to a world he owed so much.

Now I understand you Charles, why you played the maître d

You were teaching me the worthlessness of High Society.

Indeed you're right, my Lady, you've done more than all Debretts

With one kind word and a smile, so please have no regrets

By the way my cuisine is famous, from here to Timbuctoo

And in every one of my restaurants there's a table reserved for you.

JAMES AND THE CYBERDRAGON

James Bartholomew gazed at his handiwork and exclaimed excitedly, 'I'm going to be famous'.

All Bekky could do was nod dumbly as she goggled at what was sitting on top of her brother's computer, slime from its scales oozing down the screen. Eventually she stuttered, 'But...it looks so real. The eyes, that tail and those horrid, spiky teeth. And what's that red, smoky stuff coming out of its nostrils?'

James snorted. 'That smoky stuff's smoke, that's what it is. Haven't you seen a dragon before?'

'Course I have, but only in books. I've never seen a...what you call it..? A Virtual Reality dragon before.'

James swivelled round and glowered at his nine-year-old twin sister. 'Virtual Reality, Huh!'

He gestured towards the tiny but perfectly formed prehistoric beast, now swinging its head from side to side menacingly, 'Meet Cyberdragon, a real, live limb-ripping, skull-crunching, blood-drooling monster.' James added importantly, 'And I made it.'

'What do you mean, you made it? Nobody can make a real dragon.' Bekky added nervously, 'Can they..?'

'Well I can. And now I'm going to be richest and famousest person in the world. I'll be on the tele, social media and in all the papers...'

Bekky eyed the creature warily. It certainly looked real. She noticed it was now regarding them both thoughtfully, much as a crocodile might size up its next meal. It was a good job, thought Bekky, that it was so tiny. About the size of a lizard. Although...funny that...was it her imagination, or was it getting bigger?

She forced her attention back to James. 'How...how did you make it?' She asked, still not totally convinced.

James scratched his head. 'Well...I'm not <u>actually</u> sure. I was in Klik and Create and decided to design the nastiest, horridest, scariest, ugliest, evilest, monster I could think of.

'When I'd finished, it just jumped out of the screen and sort of...appeared.'

Bekky looked back at the product of her brother's creative talent. It WAS getting bigger. A few minutes ago it had been the size of a fat worm with legs. Now, it had assumed the proportions of a large mouse.

She felt her mouth grow dry. Supposing it went on getting bigger and ended up as tall as a tower block? And was a ferocious devourer of human flesh?

'James,' she whispered urgently. 'It's growing.' James glanced casually at the creature and his brows knit in puzzlement. 'Er...Hmmm...I think you're right. It's probably all the Kitekat it's eaten.'

'Kitekat?' Said Bekky. 'You haven't been feeding it Bunter's catfood?'

'Well I had to,' said James defensively. 'Matter of fact, I used the last two tins in the cupboard.' Seeing Bekky's face suffusing red with indignation, James hurried on, 'I couldn't have the world's first human-made dragon dying of starvation could I?'

'But what about Bunter? He should have been fed by now, he'll be starving.'

Bunter was the family cat. He was fat and contented and was unrecognisable as the skinny, black stray which had followed their mother home a year ago.

Mrs Bartholomew had christened it Bunter after the storybook character who was overly fond of his food. Their pet was always hungry and ate at least two tins of catfood a day.

In her anxiety over Bunter's next meal Bekky had forgotten James's dragon, or whatever it was. She noticed it had now expanded to the size of a guinea pig. If it went on growing this fast it would be as tall as a horse by morning, she mentally calculated.

James shifted in his chair. '...Um...I think perhaps we'd better tell mum,' he said uneasily.

They both dashed for the door, James beating Bekky down the stairs by barely an arm's length. Mrs Bartholomew was doing the ironing in the front room.

'Now what are you two in such a hurry about?' She asked absent-mindedly as she remembered she had to go down to the corner shop and get some more catfood. She could have sworn there had been two tins left. Bunter hadn't been fed today. He'd be starving.

'James's made a real, live monster,' Bekky blurted out breathlessly.

'I'm going to be famous...' James added importantly.

'But it's growing ever so fast...' interrupted Bekky.

'So we thought we'd better tell you,' finished James, 'In case you needed to call the zoo or something.'

Mrs Bartholomew looked at James and sighed. Him and his computer games. 'Zoos are for real animals, not the product of your over-active imagination, young man,' she chided.

'But it's not imaginary. It's a real monster. It just...sort of...materiamised,' James said lamely.

'And I suppose it's got red smoke coming from its nostrils, too,' said their mother.

'Yes, yes, it has,' brother and sister chorused, jumping up and down excitedly.

Mrs Bartholomew switched the iron off at the plug. 'In that case, you two, I'd better have a look before it sets fire to the bedroom.'

When they arrived at the top of the stairs James noticed with alarm that he had left the door ajar. Mrs Bartholomew pushed it open. 'Well, where is this fire-breathing monster?' She asked disbelievingly.

James looked round. There was the computer, on top of the desk where he had left it. But, of his dragon there was no sign. It had completely disappeared. Bekky looked across at him. So he had been teasing after all. But how had he made it look so realistic?

'But it was right there,' protested James, desperately pointing. 'It had rows of ugly teeth and breathed red smoke, just like you said.'

'Another of your jokes, Eh?' His mother said reproachfully. 'A real, live dragon, indeed...Just for that you can pop to the shop and get some catfood for Bunter.'

At the mention of his name, there came a soft <u>meouw</u>, from the direction of James's chair. All three swivelled to look at the family pet.

'What on earth..?' Exclaimed their mother.

They all stared, transfixed. In time with each contented purr little wisps of fiery, red smoke drifted from the sides of Bunter's   mouth.

SHREDDING THE EVIDENCE

He's managed to endure a lifetime of scorn, thanks to his twin retreats - the library and his garden. The prospect of a future trapped in close confinement with a nagging machine has turned Stanley's thoughts to murder. More precisely, a brutal, cold-blooded - and perfect - execution.

And down the garden path comes his victim, though of course she doesn't suspect anything. Mildred has long since abandoned the notion of loving and respecting her husband. She blames Stanley for her broken dreams.

Instead of achieving status and a fat pension Stanley is about to end an undistinguished local government career with a whimper.

Her peevish tone is typical of the way she addresses Stanley these days. 'I've said it before and I'll say it again: you're obsessed with your rotten garden. I might as well not be here...' Stanley's heard it all before. He looks up with a resigned smile and methodically collects his tools. It's method that will make him a successful murderer.

'I'll just put these in the shed, my dear, and I'll be in...' Having asserted herself over her spineless spouse, Mildred snorts and turns on her heel. Even her rear view, as she disappears towards the house, radiates a righteous martyrdom.

All Stanley wants out of life is to spend his retirement contentedly in his garden. And this is the future he intends to have.

He's examined his plan from every angle. And Google has been handy, too, to check the odd detail he wasn't sure of. He's now certain he can kill his dear Mildred quickly, cleanly and humanely. And then dispose of her body - perhaps remains might be a better description - in a way that they'll never be found.

And Stanley loves the irony that Mildred, implacable enemy of his beloved plot, will at last find herself being a useful contributor to his horticultural ambitions. Stanley's unwitting accomplice in his break for freedom is Bob Gibson. Bob's a landscape gardener and lives with his wife, Joan, just down the road from the Greenwoods. Bob's been the nearest thing to a friend that Stanley's had over the years. Bob's always felt sorry for Stanley, because of Mildred.

'I'll only want it for an afternoon. I'll have all the branches sawn off and ready. Then all I've got to do is feed them into the shredder. It'll only take me an hour or so,' Stanley said to Bob yesterday.

Bob shakes his head uncertainly. 'I'm not sure Stan. It's been making a funny noise recently. And, in any case you do realise that an industrial tree shredder's not like your garden variety - it's a hell of a lot bigger for one thing. It'll grind up branches as thick as a man's thigh and turn them into chippings and sawdust. It's a highly dangerous piece of machinery.'

Stanley stifles a smile and replies earnestly, 'I've helped you with it a few times, Bob, so I know what it's like. The point is, instead of paying someone to haul away my cuttings I want to turn them into a useful mulch for my roses and shrubs. I'll be careful.' And, almost as an afterthought, Stanley leans a little closer to Bob's ear, 'I'll tell you a secret Bob. The fact is...well... Mildred and I have been having a few differences, lately. You know how it is. Anyway...she's going away for a long weekend to visit some relatives in Scotland and...well...I'm pruning the trees as a surprise and a welcome-home present. That's why I need to get on with the job tomorrow, while she's gone.'

Bob looks at Stanley's eager expression and shrugs.

'OK Stan, I'll bring the shredder round tomorrow afternoon and leave the truck with it. That way, after you've finished, the chippings can be shovelled off the back, straight into sacks ready for spreading.'

Bob shakes his head in admiration. Despite what Mildred puts poor old Stan through, the old codger still loves her and wants to give her a surprise.

Bob waves goodbye and Stanley retreats into his toolshed. Once again, he sharpens the kitchen knife - the one with the 5-inch blade - one last time to make certain it's capable of a swift kill.

Stanley's read that anyone stabbed cleanly through the heart dies quickly and quietly. And there's very little blood so long as you leave the knife in place until well after death.

He wipes the blade carefully on his gardening trousers and thinks through his plan one last time. Then, satisfied, he shouts down the garden to his wife, who's in the kitchen. 'Mildred my love can you come into the shed for a moment, please.'

'What is it now? I'm on the phone, can't it wait?' She shouts back.

'When you've finished, dearest. I've got a special surprise for you.'

Mildred is intrigued. She finishes her phone conversation and walks down the path, ready to pour another dose of scorn onto her husband's head if she's made the trip for nothing. She walks into the gloom, where Stanley's waiting.

'Who was it on the phone, dear?' Stanley enquires, giving his voice an extra measure of submissiveness.

'Oh, no-one important,' Mildred replies. Then her voice takes on a harder edge. 'Now what is it you want? It's alright for you - pottering out here every spare moment. I've been on my feet all day and now I'm right in the middle of getting supper ready. So, what's the surprise.'

Stanley pauses for a moment. The words he'd been rehearsing assemble themselves joyously in his head. Then, in a snarl worthy of any Hollywood gangster, he replies. 'Just this, you selfish, domineering, insensitive, unloving, nagging, cold-hearted, hateful old cow.' Stanley raises the knife and plunges it downwards with all his strength.

Mildred is astounded. Her Stanley's never even raised his voice to her before, let alone abuse her in such a fashion. Her reeling mind is scarcely aware of the sharp pain in her chest.

Suddenly she's very tired. Her legs are too weak to hold her up. Everything around her is swimming. Her eyes are misting over. She wants to say something to Stanley but nothing comes out. Slowly she slides to the wooden floor.

Her last thought before she dies is to wonder why Stanley has taken everything out of the chest freezer to stack them on the workbench. All the food will be ruined...

Stanley looks down at his late wife. He's pleased to note that the only evidence of blood is on Mildred's blouse, which has a red stain spreading like a small inkblot outwards from the knife handle.

As he proceeds with his plan, he talks to himself checking each stage of the operation.

'Remove her clothes very carefully...Not a drop of blood on the floor or anywhere else my lad...Then burn the lot in the incinerator, which I'll then load into Bob's grinder tomorrow, with the...er...other material.'

He makes a neat bundle of Mildred's clothes and then places his hands under her naked armpits. He heaves until her torso hangs over the lip of the empty freezer. Now, he tips her still warm and pliant corpse in and arranges her into a sitting position. Once she is just a frozen carcase, he needs her to be in a shape that will be easy to dismember. Stanley closes the lid with a satisfied sigh.

Now, all he has to do is wait until Bob delivers his industrial-sized mincing machine, by which time Mildred will be as stiff as a side of English mutton.

Still muttering to himself, Stanley checks the final stages of the operation. 'After burning her clothes I finish off cutting enough branches to give a sizable load of chippings.

'Then I come back in here and saw Mildred up into branch size pieces before feeding them, chunk by chunk, along with the rest of the wood, into the shredder. And, Hey Presto, Mildred's reduced to a pile of humus chips which, mixed with the wood, will go nicely round the roses.

'Goodbye, Mildred my precious. And hello, peace and freedom.'

Stanley collects up the scattered contents of the freezer and puts them into two bags ready to transport to the other freezer in the house. No point in wasting good food, he thinks. He puts the shed door on the latch and tramps up the garden path to the kitchen to wash his hands. He won't be removing the knife from his wife's body until her blood's frozen solid.

He'll tell their friends that Mildred has left him and is staying with relatives in Scotland until they sort out the divorce. 'Now, it's only a matter of sawing up the body when it's solid and Bob's shredder will do the rest...'

Later that day Bob's battered Nissan truck draws up outside the house. Bob and Joan get out. Bob heads for the front door while Joan takes the path round the side of the house to the garden at the back. Stanley opens the front door and greets Bob with a warm smile. Bob looks apologetic.

'Sorry about this, Stan. But my bloody shredder's gone and packed up on me so I can't let you have it tomorrow. Apparently the gearing's gone inside. There are no spare parts locally so it could take weeks to fix.

Bob doesn't notice that Stanley's face, like that of Stanley's late wife, is frozen in shock.

Stanley holds on to the door frame as his legs threaten to give way. 'The other reason we've called,' Bob continues oblivious to Stanley's rising panic, 'is to borrow some bread. Joan rang Mildred earlier and Mildred said you'd got a spare loaf we could have.'

Stanley pulls himself together and, ignoring the two bags with the contents of the shed freezer, turns towards the kitchen to see what there is in the bread bin.

Bob calls after him, 'No need to make yourselves short for tea, Stan. Mildred told Joan there's a couple of loaves in your freezer in the shed. She said for Joan to go straight there and help herself...

'Stan...Stan...Are you feeling alright? You've gone a very funny colour...'

Bob and Stan stare at each other in horror as a terrified scream pierces the air...

COME INTO MY PARLOUR...

'Darling, you don't believe me but I know I'm going to die tomorrow,' Samantha James told her husband across the breakfast table. She held up her hand before he could protest. 'I've left you all my worldly goods - except for a small bequest to charity.'

Robert James sighed in exasperation at his wife's morbid pronouncement. He looked over the top of his Daily Telegraph, keeping his finger on the share prices.

'Now, now Sam, sweetheart, you'll get into one of your states again.' He peered back at the columns of figures. He'd checked and re-checked the portfolio a dozen times. Thanks to his shrewd investment skills his wife's legacy was now worth well over five million.

He smiled to himself. They were going to have a wonderful future. The two of them, still very much in love.

They'd have the world at their feet. Just one final gamble...

Sam's voice intruded into his reverie. 'Darling, you haven't heard a word I've said, have you --?'

'--I'm sorry Sam. I was just thinking about your shares. If we cashed in the lot now, do you know how much you'd be worth?'

His wife brushed the question aside. Her voice took on a petulant note, 'I wish you'd take me seriously. I may not be here after tomorrow.'

Robert reached for her hand and squeezed it gently. He sighed inwardly. At times it took all his patience, living with Sam's...lapses. But, over the three years of their marriage, he had coped with everything. Well, everything except her fear of spiders...But, he hoped, even they wouldn't be troubling her soon.

'For the last time my love, you are not going to die. Look at you, you're a picture of health. And you've got everything a woman could possibly want - beauty, brains, and a husband who loves you very much. And' - he gestured at the finance pages - 'not many couples still in their twenties can say they've got no money worries.'

Robert was right, she thought. And they had status in the community, too, with her husband's partnership in the town's most respected firm of solicitors.

Yes, they had everything. And yet...She clenched her fingers until they hurt. Her "darkness" was spoiling things again. It had first come when she was little. It felt like a black fog embracing her soul. And every time it came, someone close to her died. First it was her father, then her gran and then Charmian, her best friend, the fog enfolded her just before that terrible drowning accident.

Her "darkness" came almost like a warning, she thought. And now it was inside her again, brought on by that silly visit to a clairvoyant.

She shook her head, 'I'm sorry Robert but I just can't get out of my mind what happened at Madame Petulengro's --'

'--Samantha, dearest, we have been over this a dozen times. Fortune-telling is pure mumbo-jumbo. It was supposed to be a bit of fun. I'd never have suggested it if I thought it would bring on one of your...your...moods--'

'--Not moods, Robert, let's use the proper psychiatric

term—bi-polar. Isn't that what that consultant called it?'

Robert walked round the table putting his face next to hers. 'He said it was a mild form of bi-polar and nothing that couldn't be cured by time and a caring husband.'

Squeezing her shoulders playfully, he changed the subject. 'That Madame Petulengro's going to end up in court under the Trades Descriptions Act. I bet she's no more a Romany than I am. She's probably a middle-aged, bored stay-at-home making a bit of pin money.'

Samantha relaxed against him and smiled in spite of herself, 'You might be a lawyer but you wouldn't make a very good witness. Madame Petulengro is nowhere near middle-aged. And she could well come from gypsy stock - didn't you notice how beautiful she was? Those dark eyes, high cheekbones and lovely features--'

'--Tush, I didn't notice because I only have eyes for you, my darling...' Robert kissed her hair.

'I know you're trying to steer me off the subject but I still can't stop this feeling I have...And , well, you saw her expression. One minute she was smiling into that crystal ball thing and the next she seemed...well...shocked. Then

she wouldn't say anything and I had to practically drag it out
of her--'

'--Sam, that's enough. You're imagining things.' It was
just as the consultant had warned, he thought. She was
becoming obsessive. And if one of these phases coincided
with her spiders phobia, she could go temporarily right
over the edge.

His wife shook her head. 'But, she seemed to know so
much about me. It was eerie. And then she finally admitted
she could see nothing in my life after tomorrow. And with
those...those...warnings I get ...Oh Robert I'm frightened.'

Robert began to be alarmed at the turn the
conversation was taking. He must steer her away from this
dangerous introspection. He held her and stroked her
soothingly. He must be supportive...just like he was over
those bloody spiders. How had the doctor described it? An
irrational fear. Quite common, he'd said. But in extreme
cases some arachnophobes became momentarily deranged
when confronted by one.

And Sam had a sixth sense if a spider was anywhere
near her. She'd suddenly leap to her feet and dash from the
room screaming - literally screaming. Even pictures of

spiders made Sam cover her eyes. If she ever saw a live one while cooking with something like boiling fat...He shivered. In the wrong circumstances Sam could be a positive danger to herself, he thought.

He pulled her gently to him. 'I'll tell you what I'll do, I'll take tomorrow off. You can lie in bed all day and I'll stand guard...'

'Samantha smiled at his clumsy attempt to reassure her. He was such a perfect husband. She swore she'd make a real effort to conquer her nerves. If she could just get through tomorrow...

The following evening Robert arrived home an hour earlier than usual. He put his arm round her protectively. 'Darling, that feeling of apprehension you've had. Well, I caught the end of something on the car radio which really shocked me but could explain everything about your...er...presentiments.' His wife looked at him curiously. 'It was all about Madame Petulengro. She's...well...she's just died in an accident. The newsreader said witnesses had seen her car suddenly accelerate at the closed railway crossing, smash through the barrier and straight into the path of the inter-city express. No passengers, or anyone else it seems, were hurt – just Madame Petulengro.'

Sam looked puzzled. "You mean the clairvoyant I saw yesterday has been killed? I don't understand.'

Robert said, 'I know it's hard to take it. I've been trying to get my head round it myself all the way home. But the reason Madame Petulengro couldn't see anything in your life after the next day is now obvious - because her life had ceased to exist. The poor woman naturally assumed the crystal ball was blank - or whatever happened to it - because you were going to die. But, it was she who had no future.'

Robert pressed on, 'And your "darkness" was right. Something terrible was going to happen. But not to you.'

Robert sat beside his wife. She buried her head in his neck. 'Oh, Robert, how ghastly for the woman and her family. It makes you realize how life can be hanging by a thread but we don't know it. It's so precious. I realize my fears and phobias must be so trying for you.' Her face brightened. 'Let's do what you suggested. Let's cash in all my stocks and spend the money on us. We should share as many memorable experiences as we can, while we can.'

Robert took her in his arms. 'I've been thinking the same thing.' He smiled, 'Who wants to spend the rest of his life in a dusty old office when he's got a beautiful, clever, rich wife to keep him in a manner he's not accustomed to.'

He patted a cushion and leaned her back against it. 'Cooking dinner is my treat this evening. You just sit there and dream...'

Sam stretched and thought of poor Madam Petulengro, or whatever her real name was. She shuddered. What was the news saying now? She wondered. She reached out to switch the radio on as Robert popped his head round the door. His face froze.

He strode to her side and covered her hand with his. 'Don't darling, it'll only upset you.' He looked at his watch. 'I've got a better idea. While I exercise my culinary skills you take my car and pop down to the off-licence, you know the one just over the level crossing - not the one where the accident happened because the road will be closed - the other one, and get a bottle of bubbly to celebrate our momentous decision.' He drew her to her feet. 'Here are the keys. It'll only take two minutes.'

An hour later Robert poured himself a glass of the best champagne. This was how it was going to be from now on. Now that he was a multi-millionaire.

He switched on the radio, to see if there was any news on the accident...

'...And tonight's main story is the tragic death of a woman motorist who drove into the path of an inter-city express. Witnesses said the woman halted as the railway crossing lights began flashing. But then she appeared to lose control. The car smashed through the automatic barrier and was hit by a London-bound train travelling at over 60mph...

'...Police have declined to identify the driver until next of kin have been informed, but she's been locally identified as the wife of a prominent local solicitor...'

Robert smiled to himself, twirling the glass in his hand. The telephone rang. It was the call he'd been waiting for.

A familiar voce said silkily, 'The plan worked perfectly, Robert darling. The crossing closed just as she arrived. I walked across the road to her car door and when she wound down the window she looked thunderstruck – as if she'd seen a ghost.

'And then when I dangled that giant plastic spider in front of her face...'

Robert sighed with satisfaction. His last gamble had come off. His wife, prone to irrational behaviour, had been killed in a tragic accident. People would be so sympathetic. From now on there would be just him and the woman he adored, sharing their dreams together.

He spoke softly into the phone. 'Yes, just as we predicted, my darling.' Robert took another sip of the pale, bubbly liquid in his glass. 'Or should I say just as your crystal ball foretold, Madame Petulengro…

PUNISHMENT

I've just died. And I'm really amazed at what my last thoughts were. I mean there I was, the car spinning towards oblivion, and all I can think of is how angry Steph's going to be when I'm late for lunch.

You'd think that when a soul's about to embark on its final adventure, the brain could come up with something a little more…profound than overdone lamb chops. I'm not religious but I always harboured a childlike faith that God, or Allah, or Buddha, or whoever runs things on the other side, would make crossing from this world into the next a bit of an occasion. That's why I'm floating about here feeling - cheated. No heavenly choirs, no ethereal beings to guide me to my celestial niche. Nothing dramatic at all.

Of course, you can't see me can you? I'm up here, near the ceiling looking down on myself in that bed there. Can you see me? Yes? Good, we can have a proper tete a tete now. I'm not going to go on about this trivia business except to warn you - don't expect a fanfare of trumpets and the Hallelujah Chorus when your turn comes. But, I wouldn't want you to think that dying's all negative. There IS a positive side. For a start the actual state of being dead isn't at all bad. So far, it feels very peaceful: like floating in a warm Caribbean sea and looking forward to a carefree al fresco lunch. Know what I mean?

I haven't been dead for long though, so things could take a turn for the worse, I suppose. I didn't explain properly how I got here did I? Lets recap a minute. I was driving along the M4 and the next thing I knew there was a hell of a bang and I was watching myself from above. It was really weird. It was like being a detached observer at someone else's disaster. It was at the moment I knew I was going to die that my brain fired off its last emergency SOS about being late for lunch. Then, trapped in a heap of buckled metal, plastic and glass, I (or what was left of me) came to a final shrieking halt on the hard shoulder. I could see there was no hope. I had to be dead. And then I felt a sort of sadness - for him... I mean me... and those who'd got to clear up the mess.

And poor old Steph still fuming over another spoiled lunch. To be perfectly honest I think I must have fallen asleep at the wheel. That's the last time I go on an all night binge, I can tell you. Where was I? Oh yes. I was saying it's not so bad being dead. But it does make you wonder. What was it all for? All those years of worry? First school exams and teenage spots. Then marriage and the mortgage. And school fees and outdoing next door's latest acquisition. It all seems so trivial from the perspective of being...well...dead.

They say you never appreciate what you had until you've lost it. It's absolutely true, I can tell you. And I'm living proof...er...I mean, there's so much in the world to bring real joy to the human heart - apple blossom in the Spring, the liquid song of the thrush, the excitement of the children with their first hampster. Don't miss it and pile up a lot of regrets, like me. I know I should have cuddled Steph more often; told her that I loved her. I wonder how much she'll miss me? I suppose she'll be quite a catch now. My insurances'll pay the mortgage off and there'll be more than enough to fund the kids through school. And leave her a tidy sum to live on.

Well, good luck to her I say. She deserves a second chance. So, what happens now? I can't go on through eternity hanging around here. I wish someone would come for me. I say come for...I don't know what the procedure is. All I seem to be doing is floating invisibly and looking down on the late, yet to be lamented, James Colin Hargreaves. Poor old bugger. Well, not old. Forty-two's not old. But I'm - he's - not going to get to 43 that's for sure. And here's a late bulletin...I'm beginning to feel a bit sentimental now. Is a discarnate spirit supposed to have feelings? Just looking at what's left of me is triggering off all kinds of emotions.

Shhh! Someone's coming. It's really strange. I can see everything that's going on but they can't see me. It's like one of those 'Out of Body Experiences' you read about. Hmmm! I'm privileged. TWO doctors and TWO nurses have positively erupted into the room. They've gone straight to that obscene pile of flesh and bones that used to be me. Oh, No! I think they are trying to bring it back to life. How could that crushed mess ever live again? I'm feeling a bit strange. My sense of peaceful floating's draining away.

I can feel myself being sucked back towards those ghastly remains...I can see every broken bone...the caved-in chest, the crushed spine, how could it ever live a normal life? Oh, God, No! It wants me back inside it. Don't make me go back. I can't bear pain. I couldn't stand the suffering. I couldn't ever be what I used to be. I want to stay here. Please let me stay floating in my warm, secure sea of peace.

Now I'm scared. I'm feeling crushed. I'm being drawn back into that broken carcase and I can't breathe. If there is a God, don't punish me. Don't punish me, God! I haven't been that bad have I? And what about Steph and the children? How are they going to cope with the grotesque abomination that I would be? A God who cared would never do this to his children. Call yourself a loving God?. I'm pleading with you. Please...please...don't make me live...

ALPHA-RHYTHMS AND CYBERDRAGONS

I haven't been on Spice honest. But they're all round us. But you can't see them. I could. Well, I did, but I can't now. Jeez, I'm not making sense, am I? What I mean is: It really happened. What happened to that kid James, who you read about earlier, has happened to me. But magnified by a few extra-galactic parsecs. And I was responsible. Well, me and Klik and Create. Plus my XPS 27 7760 all-in-one desktop computer with seventh generation Intel processor and 1TB solid state drive

Not that the spec is relevant, but I tend to ramble when I'm panicking.

Panicking? Yeah, I don't think it's too strong a word to describe the iron mit clutching my entrails. What I'm trying to say is, I created a monster. No kidding. A real, live limb-ripping, skull-crunching, blood-drooling cyberdragon.

And it's going to happen to you, too. It could have already, but you won't realise it. They're all over the place. But they're invisible, except to very special people. Like me. You must think I'm crazy. But, don't tune out. Please.

I'm still not sure how I did it. But he told me before he de-materialised through the wall that it was to do with my brain and something called alpha-rhythms, or some such. But I'm getting ahead of myself.

Take a deep breath, Danny Calvino, and start at the beginning.

Calvino? Yes, my dad's Italian. He married my mum, who's as English as roast beef and Yorkshire pud. But, he's not with us any more. But my mum is. In fact we're a pretty happy family. Me, mum and my twelve-year-old sis, Sara. Where was I? Ah yes, the end of the world, as we know it.

Whoops, I didn't mean to blurt that out. I was going to be more subtle. But, now that you know...

But you don't really, do you? I'm burbling again. I think it's because I'm so shit-scared. There I've owned up. And that's a measure of the seriousness of the situation. Because

I'm not one to admit being afraid of anything. Not even Slug Warner when he's on one of his eye-tie-bashing rampages.

Lungful again. As I said, I was lost in an inter-galactic world of Klik and Create technology, dredging up every vile, stinking, corrupt, rotting, evil ingredient for a monster my imagination could produce, when it happened.

For a while the child of my psyche floated supine in the cyberworld in front of me, blood oozing from between its pointed fangs, with a whisp or two of red smoke floating from its nostrils for realism.

Then, without so much as a click on my mouse, the beast sprang into the air. I watched it ascend spacewards, craning my neck until it disappeared off the screen.

And while I was still craning, it sort of...materialised on top of my Dell. Imagine it, our eyes were inches apart as it squatted there, fixing me in an evil, yellow stare.

The green slime covering it oozed down the front of the monitor and spread like a pool across the top of my playstation. The one that mum had so personfully assembled just a fortnight ago.

Then it leapt onto a chair and started to grow. Like a balloon inflating, its red tongue flicking from side to side as its teeth, like evil stalactites and stalagmites, burst from its gums.

As you can well imagine, I was transfixed. My eyes were like billiard balls as its leathery skin creaked and the scales stretched to accommodate an expanding body. It sprouted three-toed arms and feet. Then its huge, rubbery tale slithered over the arm of the chair and disappeared under our spare bed.

I crawled over and peered into the space where our spare slippers are usually kept. There it was, my mind's creation, made flesh. I don't know how long it was we stared at each other. But my concentration broke when it spoke to me.

'Not an edifying spectacle from where I'm sitting,' it said in a superior sort of way as it scuttled into the open and leapt onto my chair.

I decided to ignore the implied insult and concentrate, instead, on figuring out whether I was asleep and having a nightmare. Or awake and having a bad trip. A healthy swig of Four-X eliminated the first possibility.

And, I realised it had been weeks since I'd indulged, so it couldn't be the second.

'I get it...' I said with a show of bravado (It hadn't worked with Slug Warner but you never knew)...'this is state-of-the-art Virtual Reality. You don't actually exist. You are a mere figment of my imagination.'

All my words achieved was a contemptuous snort. And as you'll recall from your studies of myths and legends, it's in the nature of the beast that when dragons snort, they tend to incinerate anything within jousting distance.

The heat generated by the twin tongues of flame that jetted across my bedroom pretty near incinerated my ears.

So, it got its point across. Whatever it was, it wasn't 'Virtual.' I waited uneasily as it beat an impatient tattoo on the arm of the chair with its triple claws, collecting its thoughts. I stuttered something about...a dragon...before we lapsed into companionable silence. I sat rigid and attentive while IT stared at the ceiling, idly twirling the end of its tail, lassoo-like.

Eventually, it asked, sort of rhetorically, 'How can I put this and make it easy for you to grasp, Danny?' I don't remember giving it permission to use the familiar form of my given. But I decided not to make an issue of it. It went on, 'You are us and we are you...'

Did you notice the "we"? I did. I'm quick like that.

'There are others like you, around then?' I said, keeping it casual, like.

It nodded, a yellow gleam in its eye. Oh, didn't I mention it? I say "eye" because that's all it had. Like that Cyclops character in an old black and white movie on the tele the other Saturday afternoon. I think that's where I got the idea from. Just goes to show what gets stored away in the subconscious.

I'm wandering again, aren't I? Where was I? Oh, yes. Its one eye had a sort of triumphant glint.

'You dunno the 'arf of it,' says the dragon. Then, he shot his cuff, as if looking at his watch--which is one of my little ways. 'As I speak,' he goes on, 'we are spawning across the globe, drawing energy and form from the cesspit of man's imaginings.'

For a primeval beast from another dimension, he certainly had a way with words. There aren't many handy ripostes to a statement like that. So, after a quick ponder on the options, I decided to plump for familiar territory.

'And you all live in our computers?' I enquired politely.

He looked at me wearily and shook his head in disgust. 'Haven't you been listening to a word I've said? Of course we don't live in your computers. We wouldn't fit for a start. How could this...' He pointed at his gross, ugly body...'fit into that..?' He waved a claw at my PC. 'I thought I'd made it clear,' he says, 'we exist inside you...'

I decided a humble approach might be in order. 'Sorry,' I said, 'silly of me. But I don't often get the chance to chat with a dragon...' And that's as far as I got before he snorted again, reducing my stack of old CD-ROMs to a pile of melted junk.

'What's with you and this dragon fixation?' He says. 'Dragon's are for St George and the Taffs... What you see here...' He waved a hideous appendage to indicate his scaly presence...'is the creation of your own unconscious. I am one of the multiple personalities that dwells inside Danny Calvino. I am you...'

Well I couldn't get a handle on that. How could this refugee from a Steven Spielberg production be me? He conceded it was unlikely that someone...as he put it...of my limited intelligence could grasp the concept.

'It's quite simple,' he says. Which was a laugh for a start. 'I am the embodiment of all your base thoughts.' He saw from my face I was offended. I'm no more base than the next man. He wasn't going to win any points for diplomacy, that was for sure. But he ploughed on, oblivious to any possible offence.

He said that deep in man's psyche, dark desires slop about. But usually they stay buried. Now though, thanks to computer graphics and Klik and Create programs, these yearnings were being given form. And these forms were being adopted by sinister powers from the beyond.

It's something to do with unusual brain patterns caused by you and me spending large chunks of our waking moments staring into computer screens. The concentration used in conjuring up our fantasies, is being hi-jacked.

'So, you and your mates are popping out of PC's all round the world?', I helpfully suggested.

'Well...yes and no...' he says.

'Blimey! You should be a politician,' I says.

He ignored my cheap jibe. He just said that, although these life forms are all around us, they were generally invisible. Naturally enough, I asked his Beastliness why I was the lucky one to get a full frontal.

He went all superior again saying it was a rare phenomenon, brought on by a combination of low intelligence and the frequency of a person's alpha rhythms, or words to that effect.

He then explains to me that this combination of...ahem...low wattage and Alfy Whatsits is so rare that only one in a million actually get to witness these...um...

manifestations. Which is why I'm posting this admittedly implausible tale around The Net. As a warning, like.

As I speak these psychic Draculas are feeding off your daydreams. But as long as they can't see what's in your deep-down self they're powerless. Or that's the theory.

I know you'll think I'm a barmpot but I can't sit around and do nothing, can I? Not when the future of the human race is at stake. Oh, didn't I mention that? I should have said. Before the fruit of my loins...well not loins but you know what I mean...

Anyhow, before Danny sort of de-materialised - Oh, I decided to call him Danny. Not that I totally believe in this schizo theory, but Danny the Dinosaur makes a handy alliteration, don't you think?

Anyway, Danny said...now let me get this right...Danny said ...'The satanic side of mankind's collective unconscious is breaking free everywhere...' And that the energies released are stoking up chaos and mayhem across the world. Yeah, that's a fair representation I reckon.

Apparently, it's a bit like nuclear fission. You know, neutrons having a nervous breakdown and going into overload. Every time you and me sit at our screens and let rip with our psyches, we're creating more, evil Dannys, or Jacks or Matts or Ryans... or Jessicas, or Hannahs or Charlottes...See what I mean?

Crazy I know, but it does make sense. Think about it. Better still, look around. What do you see? Mayhem - in bucket-loads. Danny also said something about Armaggedon and the final trump. Or should that be Trump? And Nostradamus and 2021.

I asked him straight out if the end of the world was inevitable. I mean, it's not the sort of prognostication to take lying down, is it? Well, according to our friend, there is an outside chance Homo Sapiens can be saved. But it's down to you and me. And we've got to act fast. He then gave me a step-by-step guide to survival.

Funny that, though. How easy it was to get him to spill the beans. Bit like 2nd World War Rommel handing over his battle plans to Monty. But, I'm not one to look a gift horse in the mouth. Danny's secret's so hush-hush it can't go on general circulation. If it did, it'll alert the enemy. That's why I'm steering clear of FB, Instagram and the like and confining this message to my blog. Only the chosen few who read it will be saved!

So, I'll send detailed instructions 'eyes-only' to you individually. I've deliberately left my contact details off this blog so I don't get a tsunami of trolls. If you want to avoid the end of your world, rush me your E-mail address now. Stupid of me, you can't do that can you, 'till you've got mine. I'm so rattled I can't think straight. What with Danny and all. Anyway, you can get me atttttttttttt

tttttttttttttttttttttttttttttttttttttttttttttttttttttttttttttttttttttttttt

tttttttttttttttttttttttttttttttt

INADMISSIBLE EVIDENCE

Picture the scene:

A little girl is skipping along a rural tree-lined street reciting quietly to herself, 'Salt...mustard...vinegar...pepper...salt...mustard...vinegar...pepper...salt...mustard...vinegar...pepper…salt...mustard...' Suddenly, the air is pierced by a terrified scream which mingles with the chimes of an ice cream van. Then both cease as if a giant hand has dropped a sound-proof dome over both, leaving the village enveloped in a quiet repose.

The scene moves to the living room of an unpretentious bungalow. There's a knock on the door, which opens immediately.

George and Christine Cooper are shown in and woman in her thirties, with an open face and a genuine smile, greets them. _Take a seat, please. I'm Sarah.' She hesitates and then adds gently, 'I know how terrible this must be for you both, I've got two children myself—'

George responds immediately, as if about to explode and ready to lash out at anyone. 'Thank you, Dr Wyatt,' he says stiffly. 'But, how could you possibly know? We're just about hanging onto our sanity.'

Christine lays a hand on George's arm as if to soothe his inner turmoil. But her voice betrays her own jangled emotions. 'When I go into Vicky's bedroom, and see all her things, it's just like she's at her nan's and...only away for the night...' She begins to sob...'And'll be back in the morning... Only she won't...she won't. She's never coming back, is she..?'

George puts his arm round his wife, drawing her close. 'Come on, darling, we mustn't give up.' He looks at Sarah. ' You see what I mean, Dr Wyatt? We're both at our wit's end.'

Sarah asks, 'What are the police saying now?'

George sighs wearily,_ 'They've done their best. But they're no further forward than they were two weeks ago.

They say it all takes time, sifting every scrap of information—'

Christine chokes back her tears, 'And meanwhile Vicky's God knows where. She could be alone somewhere, terrified. Or some monster could be...could be…' She punches the cushion in frustration._ 'My God I feel so...helpless.'

George explains, ' That's why we've come to you, Dr Wyatt. You're our last hope. If only we knew where to start looking...'

Sarah regards them both. 'Mr and Mrs Cooper, you mustn't expect too much.'

Christine pleads, ' But you have done this sort of thing before? We've read about you in the papers and you've been on television...You're a professor, too, aren't you?'

'Not exactly, Mrs Cooper. I have a PhD degree in psychology. Then I went on to study parapsychology at City University.'

'Parapsycholgy?' Says George, 'Is that another word for the Supernatural?'

'Well, sort of. It looks at things like hypnosis and telepathy. It was because I'd always had a feeling for psychic matters, I decided to specialise in that field--but as a scientist, to see if I could understand what was going on—'

'--And that led you to finding missing people..? '

'That just...happened...along the way. After I qualified, I got onto the lecture circuit. This led to some TV and radio appearances which prompted two parents--like yourselves-- to ask me for help.'

George's wife says excitedly, 'That's why we're here, Dr Wyatt. I remember reading about it at the time. What was the boy's name..? Richard...um...'

Sarah interjects, '...Richard Greenwood. As you know, he'd been kidnapped. The police had tried--unsuccessfully-- to find him. By using, shall we say, unconventional techniques, I managed to pinpoint the house and the cellar in which Richard was being held and he was rescued unharmed.'

Christine asks, 'But, how did you know? How did you know the exact place to look?'

'Well...And this is where we enter realms that most people find...er...difficult to comprehend.' She adds lightly, ' I do myself at times. I used a technique called psychometry. I held Richard's shoe, which had come off when his abductor had grabbed him, and sensed what had happened and where Richard had been taken. I know it seems fantastic, but sometimes I see pictures in my mind of actual events that have happened.'

Christine says imploringly, 'If only you could do the same for us, Dr Wyatt. We'd do anything...pay anything...'

Sarah smiles. 'That won't be necessary. Have you brought Vicky's skipping rope with you..?'

Our action moves to the busy ops room at Wessex police headquarters where Chief Superintendent Jack Brodie is showing round high flyer and newly arrived Det Inspector Adam Rycroft.

'Last stop on our Cook's tour, Ryecroft. The operations room--nerve centre of our unremitting war against the darker reaches of the criminal mind. ' He chortles, 'Could teach the Met or NCA a thing or two, eh?'

'Well, sir...'

'No, don't bother to answer. You probably think it's all pretty small beer.' Brodie lowers his voice and continues pugnaciously, 'But let me make something quite clear to you, Ryecroft, from Day One of your attachment here: I'll stand for no pyrotechnics...'

'Sorry, sir..?'

'You know exactly what I mean. I want to see no demonstrations of your celebrated contempt of authority, no flying in the face of established police procedures. In short, I'm a by-the-book man and that's how you're going to play it here.'

Brodie gets into his stride. 'You might have cracked a few cases but, unfortunately for you, you've trodden on too many toes in the process. That's why you've been assigned to me for...er...rehabilitation. So, message received Inspector?'

Adam replies levelly, 'Message received, sir.'

At this point the two are joined by a slim, lightly-built woman of about thirty and Brodie says heartily, 'Ah, right on cue. Allow me to introduce your assistant, Inspector· Sergeant Zoe Sinclair, this is Inspector Adam Ryecroft.'

Adam tries to hide his pleasure at the sight of an attractive colleague of the opposite sex who seems to be regarding him in the same way, 'Pleased to meet you sergeant.'

'Likewise, Sir.'

Brodie says, 'Inspector Ryecroft's joining us for a while to get the feel of a rural force. As you know I've decided he should take over the Vicky Cooper case while Inspector Symes is at the National Crime Agency. And as you were Symes's assistant, you'll help Mr Ryecroft hit the ground running.' He turns to Adam 'And Ryecroft...I expect a quick result on this one. The media's saying we've gone off the boil. And the Home Office have been bending my ear...So crack on, eh? Well, I'll leave you in Sergeant Sinclair's capable hands.' He adds with a note of steel in his voice, 'And keep me in touch with your progress, Inspector._ In fact a daily report please, first thing. On my desk. By the book, eh?'

Adam replies sardonically, 'Absolutely. By the book, sir. ' He sighs. 'Well sergeant, I suppose you'd better brief me.'

We now join the clientele of a busy restaurant. There are a murmur of voices, a clatter of cutlery and occasional laughter. The head waiter bows deferentially and greets, in a lilting Italian accent, two new arrivals, 'Sir Francis...and Lady Galbraith. Welcome back to the Topo D'Oro. I cannot remember the last time you lunched here. You have been sorely missed. But, sir, now that you are an important government minister you must spend so much time in London, is that not so?'

Sir Francis replies modestly, 'Carlo, you always were a flatterer. I am a mere junior functionary. However, a more elevated role may come my way in the fullness of time. So, in anticipation of that prospect, a bottle of your best champagne, please.'

Lady Galbraith, or Rachel as she was known before her husband had a knighthood bestowed upon him, said quietly,

'A discreet table if that's possible, Carlo. I don't feel like socialising today...'

'Your wish, Lady Galbraith, is my command.' After being seated at a corner table which had a view of the room but which was softly-lit enough to discourage prying eyes, Rachel says, 'I'm finding it so difficult. To carry on as if nothing's happened. When...when...'

Francis pats her hand and says soothingly, 'Darling, we must. We can't turn the clock back. We've got to behave normally. Now do as I do, force it out of your mind. Remember, The Home Office is practically in the bag. We've got to look to the future. We mustn't let anything jeopardise it...even...that...' He lets the sentence fall into the empty air between them.

'But it's all so horrible. I still can't believe it.'

'Rachel It's been terrible for you. Believe me, I understand. But it was nobody's fault and it's happened and we've now just got to get on with our lives. We both agreed that, didn't we?'

Rachel sighs,_ 'Sometimes, Francis, I wonder if I know you at all...'

Francis replies evenly, 'Rachel, my darling. I'm sure the best way to heal the wounds is to get back to some kind of normality. It's been two weeks now. And every day that goes by...the nightmare will fade. So come on, old girl, you must be strong for all our sakes. Call me pompous if you like, but there's a destiny to fulfill and we mustn't let something we can do nothing about get in the way.' He adds persuasively, 'Just think of it darling...The Home Office and then... poised for Number Ten.'

Rachel shudders, 'I think I want to move, Francis. I can't stand the thought of what's just across the yard—'

'--Move? Well...I tell you what, after I've got the Home Office. We'll discuss it then, OK?

'I suppose so...'

Francis pours some champagne into her glass as he recollects his recent meeting with Her Majesty's First Minister, Arthur Boyd. 'Now have some fizz while I tell you what the PM said. First he asked me would I be interested in the Home Office. Would I be interested? He knew damn well I'd been angling for it for months.'

'So what did you say?'

'I told the old goat that I'd, of course, be willing to serve the Government in whatever capacity my talents were best suited.'

'And what did the "old goat" reply?'

'He said he felt--patronising bastard--I'd served my apprenticeship in all the right areas and that, as long as there wasn't any skeleton in our cupboard that was going to come rattling out to embarrass the Government, I could expect the Home Office "in the not-too-distant-future." So you can see how important it is darling, to keep everything on an even keel.'

Rachel looks at her husband thoughtfully, ' Yes...Francis...Are you sorry now you married me?'

'Sorry that I..? _Of course not, darling. How could you possibly think that? You've been the perfect wife. If I ever do make it to the top it'll be you I have to thank.'

'But if all this blows up in our faces, it'll be my fault.'

Francis says urgently, 'No-one knows, remember? Between us we've always managed to bail him out of every wretched scrape--.'

--'Except the last one. I'm sorry, I really will try to put it out of my mind. But seeing him standing there holding that little girl's teddy bear. And then—'

--'Panda'.

'What--?'

Francis corrects his wife, as if being specific will somehow improve things. 'Panda--it was a toy Panda. Darling, this may sound harsh but Jason was a wrong 'un from the start. Some people are like that. However hard their parents try, they revert to type in the end. You did your best...And if anyone's to blame it's me. When I married you and became his step-father, I should have exercised a bit more control. Instead, I ignored all the signs--his drug-taking, petty theft, his sexual shenanigans. He was wild and it was as much my fault as anyone's that things turned out as they did.'

Rachel said uncertainly, 'I know we've got to put it behind us, but it doesn't seem right; us not saying anything...hiding the truth. It should all be brought into the open...'

'Darling, that's out of the question. You know that. It just can't be...All we need is time. Everyone needs time...Then everything will be alright, you'll see. Now, try to forget it. Starting right now. Ok?'

Rachel sighs. 'I'm not convinced, but OK.'

Francis picks up his glass and speaking softly says, 'A toast: To us. And here's to the wife of the future Prime Minister...'

Meanwhile, as the Galbraiths construct around them a semblance of normality which belies the inner fears they both feel, we re-join Sarah who has switched into intuitive mode. 'This is the rope Vicky had with her when she disappeared?'

Christine replies, 'Yes. The police gave it back after all their forensic tests.' She adds bitterly, 'They found absolutely nothing. No fingerprints on the handle, no hairs caught in the fibres, not even blood. Nothing.'

George fills in the picture. 'They said they found it by the side of the road out in the country. There were a few chips on the handles, as though it had fallen, or had been thrown, out of a moving vehicle.'

Christine looks eagerly into Sarah's eyes. 'And you say you're going to use it to sense where Vicky is?'

'If I can, yes. As I said, it's called psychometry. The word was coined by an American professor last century. His theory was that all objects record emotions and events around them, rather like a camcorder or memory stick. So what I'm going to do now is concentrate on the rope...try to tune myself into any impressions Vicky might have left.'

As she speaks Sarah's voice flattens out and becomes a monotone. 'And let Vicky's emotions speak to me...Through the last thing she was holding when she disappeared...'

Vicky's parents become transfixed as Sarah's demeanour becomes more and more séance-like. 'I sense a childlike trust...and happiness...I'm skipping along the pavement...Mummy's given me some money for an ice cream...It's a lovely warm evening...'

As Sarah talks, the ticking of the long-clock in the corner of the room fills the silences as she takes on the persona of a child. She begins to chant the salt, mustard skipping rhyme. Suddenly she stops and both Christine and George look on in horror as Sarah puts up her hands as it to ward of a blow and screams until there's no air left in her lungs.

In a packed bar in the Three Ravens Public House Adam and Zoe settle themselves round a small table whose top is stained by years of spilt drinks.

Adam lays his purchases down in front of his young assistant, 'There. Orange juice and a packet of bacon and onion-flavoured for you and a nourishing pint of Best for me. Now, let's see if I've got it right, sergeant.' Adam screws up his face and half closes his eyes as he tries to recall the exact details of what he's learned. 'A five-year-old girl pesters her mother for an ice cream. Eventually, mum gives in and bungs the kid a couple of quid and lets her walk fifty yards up the street to get a Mr Softee. In the next few minutes, somewhere between the Coopers' front door and the ice cream van, young Vicky disappears off the face of the earth. Later, we find her skipping rope but not her toy panda which, apparently, she takes everywhere with her.'

Zoe reminds her boss of a salient fact. 'We did have one anonymous phone call with a man's voice saying he thinks he saw a child answering Vicky's description, in a 4-by-4, possibly a Land Rover, driving towards Uffington...'

Adam picks up the thread. 'And the road to Uffington is the same one along the side of which Vicky's skipping rope was found a few days after her disappearance?'

'Yes, sir. Which suggests the two are linked...'

'Or that someone's deliberately trying to throw us off the scent. Meaning the child could have been led off in totally the opposite direction. Either way the caller knows a lot more about young Vicky's disappearance than he's prepared to tell us face to face. Anyone recognise the man's voice?'

Zoe shakes her head. 'No sir. I took the call. Whoever it was had a handkerchief or something across the mouthpiece.'

Adam says, 'But, all the same, a clear attempt to lead us to certain conclusions. Which means the caller was no time-wasting crank...'

'Inspector Symes came to the same conclusion sir. He reckoned if someone was going to all that trouble to confuse the scent, then he must know something about the abduction. '

'Which could mean he was in on it in some way. And there's been no ransom demand?'

'No contact at all, sir.'

'Curious. Changing the subject, sergeant, how are the Coopers coping? Do they know someone else has been brought in to work on the case?'

'I don't know, sir. But, quite frankly, I don't think they'll give a damn one way or the other. They've given up on the police ever finding anything. The last I heard they'd decided to consult a parapsychologist.'

'A what?'

'A parapsychologist, Sir. You know...the occult...the supernatural.'

Adam raises his eyes to the ceiling. 'Oh my God. You mean seances and witchcraft and stuff like that? Poor devils. I suppose if you're desperate enough you'll try anything.'

Zoe shrugged, 'Well, it can't do any harm...'

Adam is aghast. 'You don't mean you believe in all that medieval mumbo-jumbo. A modern, liberated creature of the 21st Century like you.'

Zoe stands her ground. 'Have you never heard of Dr Sarah Wyatt?'

Adam snorts, 'You mean the thinking man's Mystic Meg?' He sees the puzzled expression on Zoe's face. 'Never mind. What's she got to do with our missing five-year-old?'

'Just that she lives locally and Mr and Mrs Cooper told me the last time I saw them that they intended to ask Dr

Wyatt to help them find Vicky. Even if their daughter was dead, they said, they just...needed to know.'

Adam says, 'And how's our celebrated psychic going to do that—consult a crystal ball?'

'I'm afraid I don't know, sir. All I can say is that Dr Wyatt has already successfully found a missing child. And she's worked with the police before--in locating a body.'

'Has she, by God. Which force?'

'Sussex. Remember the Jennie Butcher case? The girl abducted in her own mini?'

Adam recites what he recalls. 'Daughter of a wealthy banker and later found in a shallow grave on a common in Brighton?'

'That's the one. Well, if you remember Jennie'd been missing for 73 days. The Brighton plod had all but given up hope of finding her body. Until a journalist suggested half-jokingly that maybe it was a job for a clairvoyant. To cut a long story short, Dr Wyatt sat in Jennie's car, to sense the vibrations she said, and then told the police where she felt

Jennie's body had been buried. They found it in exactly that spot.'

'Bollocks! There's no way you'll convince me that some crackpot female going into a trance can beat honest-to-goodness coppering.' As an afterthought Adam says, 'Did they check this Dr Wyatt out? It would be easy for her to pinpoint the body, if she'd buried it there in the first place.'

Zoe says, 'That was the first thing they did apparently, all on the QT, but at the time of the abduction and murder Dr W was on a lecture tour of Canada so there's no way she could have been involved.'

Zoe takes a sip of her orange juice and jestures towards her boss. 'You don't approve of trances cracking the case, but I thought you were famous for your hunches, sir?'

Adam says, 'Hmmm. Hunches are different.'

'Are they Sir?

In the Wyatt household Sarah has finished her first psychometry session on the Vicky Cooper case and is now engaged on something familiar to us all - washing up the lunchtime dishes. Bill, her father, is drying the plates and utensils.

'Tut tut, this one fails quality control.'

'What? Oh, sorry dad. Give it back. It just needs the scourer.'

'Very sad.'

'What the state of the scourer? Yes, I suppose it is.'

'No, you chump. I mean that couple who came here this morning.'

'Ah, the Coopers. I think they've got a lot of guts. I don't know how I'd cope

if anything happened to Daniel or Katy. You can't really imagine it, can you? A child dying must be bad enough. But, for your daughter to just disappear...'

Bill says, 'I can't conceive what they must be going through. But if they needed someone to understand they came to the right person, didn't they?'

Perceiving a reference to her late husband, Sarah says, 'It's not the same, dad. Losing Tom like that was terrible. But at least I knew how he had died and why he had died. And he was an adult and he knew the risk he was taking. For the Coopers it must be much worse. They're tormented by all the horrible possibilities without really knowing...'

'What I meant was: You've been through losing the one you love in violent circumstances. Which must at least help you empathise with their suffering.'

'I suppose so. But, at least after the initial shock, I had my children and you to support me and I could grieve for Tom. But, to lose a child and not to know how or why or where. Well...'

'Were you able to help them?'

Sarah turns to her father, 'I tried. But I just don't know. They made me promise to tell them the truth about what I sensed.'

'And that was?'

'A little girl, skipping along the pavement one minute and the next...a terrible darkness. Then fear...pain...suffocation.'

'You believe she's dead, then?'

'I'm not sure. But I got this overwhelming feeling of death...I didn't tell the Coopers that, though. And I left out the fear and darkness bit, too. And after the psychometry, I tried my map dowsing. It was that which convinced me that their daughter's disappearance was associated in some way with a well. And it's on land near here. At Avonbourne, in fact.'

'Avonbourne..? Isn't that...'

'...The home of Sir Francis Galbraith, Member of Parliament and future PM if he has his way...Yes, dad, it is'

In Adam's office the phone trills and he snatches it from its rest. 'Ryecroft. ..Oh, hello sergeant....The Coopers, you say... They've what...? Do they...? OK you'd better bring them up.' He sighs and mutters to himself, 'A spell in a rural force would look good on the CV and give me a

different perspective on police work, they said. Hmmm...'
Thirty seconds later there's a knock on the door which is
pushed open immediately by Zoe 'Mr and Mrs Cooper, sir.'

Adam shakes both their hands. 'Come in. Please sit
down.' He nods at Zoe. 'Stay with us sergeant, if you would.
Mr and Mrs Cooper, Sergeant Sinclair may have told you I
have taken over the investigation into your daughter's
disappearance from Inspector Symes. My name's Ryecroft.
I've read the file on the case thoroughly. I wish I could
offer you something new but I'm afraid that, as yet, there
are no fresh developments.'

George clasps his hands together in his lap and looks
directly into Adam's eyes. 'Inspector, please don't think
we're not grateful. My wife and I know that your colleagues
have done their best to find Vicky—'.

Christine interjects impatiently, 'But the fact is it's been
over 14 days now and nothing to show for it—'

George pats his wife's knee. 'Christine, love, let me
explain to the Inspector....Inspector Ryecroft, have you got
any children?'

'Yes, a daughter. Holly. She's nine. But I don't see enough of her as I'm divorced and she lives with my ex-wife.'

'Then you must know a little of what we've been...what we're going through.'

'I know that if my daughter disappeared I wouldn't rest until I knew where she was and that she was safe.'

'Can you understand then why we're prepared to go to any lengths to find her?'

'If you mean consulting a medium, yes I know about that.'

Christine says, 'I can hear from the tone of your voice, Inspector, that you disapprove of what we've done. But, we're desperate.'

'Mrs Cooper. I'm sorry if I sounded sceptical. But...well to be blunt...I can't support the idea of a serious and painstaking police investigation being associated with...um...hocus pocus. It's a completely alien concept to an organization like the police who work on solid evidence.'

Christine leans forward and looks at Adam eagerly. 'Dr Wyatt's told us where Vicky is, Inspector. She says she thinks Vicky could be hidden in, or near, a well.' Her voice takes on an angry note. 'And she knows where this well is. Which is more than the police have been able to manage in two weeks of searching.'

Adam holds up a placatory hand. 'Now, let's all calm down. I'm sorry if I sounded dismissive. But, Mrs Cooper, how could someone who's had no connection with the investigation, or access to the notes on the case, have any idea of Vicky's whereabouts?'

George says, 'Inspector. We're not sure how. Apparently, Dr Wyatt just <u>feels</u> things. We'd heard she'd managed to find a little boy who'd been missing so we thought we've got nothing to lose. She's not what you'd expect... I mean she's so...normal. Except she's very young to be widowed...Her husband was a journalist and he was shot by a sniper in Afghanistan, apparently.'

'I didn't know that. But that still doesn't give her second sight.'

143

Zoe quickly intervenes, 'Mrs and Mrs Cooper, perhaps you could tell us what happened when you went to see Dr Wyatt.'

Christine tells how the psychic took Vicky's skipping rope – the one which had been found by the side of the road - and had just held it.

George takes up the story. 'Then she went into a sort of trance and after a while said she sensed Vicky somewhere dark. She thought at first it was a tunnel. But later she dangled this...this...pendulum thing over a map and said it wasn't a tunnel. More like a well.'

Christine interjects with a note of desperation in her voice. 'And the well was near here. And we want you to find it. Vicky could be starving. Dying...She'll be so frightened…'

Adam says quietly, 'Mr and Mrs Cooper, we're doing all we can.'

Christine begins to get emotional. 'But Dr Wyatt says she could still be alive. So you must find this well. You must, you must...'

Zoe kneels down besides her and pats her arm gently. 'Please don't upset yourself, Mrs Cooper. We really are leaving no stone unturned…'

Adam says, 'Mr Cooper, this well. Where's it supposed to be?'

'On a farm at Avonbourne.'

Zoe explains, 'Mr Cooper means Sir Francis Galbraith's land.'

'Galbraith. The junior minister? That Galbraith?'

'Yes, sir.'

Adam pauses and phones ringing in the adjoining office penetrate the silence. 'Just let me get this clear, Mr and Mrs Cooper. A clairvoyant has told you—'

'George pleads, 'No, Inspector, Dr Wyatt isn't a clairvoyant. Clairvoyants are people who claim to be in touch with the spirits of the dead. Sarah's a psychic. She has this…gift…I know it sounds mad, but she can sense events and feelings connected with inanimate objects. She says they pick up vibrations given off by emotions and these vibrations are imprinted somehow, like recordings on a video tape or flash card. She senses these recordings and somehow decodes them...'

'Well, whatever. She told you that Vicky could be found in or near a well on a local farm which, my sergeant informs me, happens to belong to a prominent member of Her Majesty's Government.'

Christine snaps, 'We don't give a damn how important this MP thinks he is. If

he's got our Vicky, we want his land searched.'

'Now just one moment' Adam admonishes. 'You can't go around accusing anyone, whoever they may be, of holding a kidnapped child, on the word of some...some...local crystal ball-gazer.'

George pleads, 'I know it's a lot to ask, Inspector. But I trust Dr Wyatt. Can't you at least see if there IS a well on Galbraith's land?'

After a pause Adam sighs heavily. 'Give me some time to talk it over with my sergeant here and I'll get back to you.'

George pleads, 'Please don't leave it long, Mr Ryecroft. I don't know how long we can remain sane with this...not knowing...hanging over us.'

Christine rises to her feet. 'We'll see ourselves out, Inspector.' She adds with a note of irony in her voice, 'We know the way. We should by now.'

After the door closes Zoe says to Adam, 'I expect the Met and the National Crime Agency had their moments, sir. But I don't suppose they produced anything quite like this.'

'You're damned right. What do you know about our local VIP?'

'Sir Francis Galbraith, knighted for his services to politics...Over 25 years in parliament...Distinguished career on the back benches...Came to the notice of Boyd who sees him as a kindred spirit. Tipped as a future Home Secretary. Then, possibly, PM. In Wessex he comes from a landowning and farming dynasty. Ditched his first wife to marry a widow, Rachel Glendinning, about seven years ago. Her family's rolling in money.'

'So, everything in the Galbraith garden's lovely. Not a cloud on their horizon, except perhaps representatives from the Wessex plod trampling all over their flowerbeds?'

Zoe smiles and continues the analogy. 'No, not quite sir. Every garden has its pests. And theirs comes in the shape of Jason, Lady Galbraith's son from her first marriage.'

'Ah, a black sheep? Or a skeleton in the cupboard?'

'At first, Jason was what some might call high spirited. Then he began to show a nasty streak. Got himself expelled from one school for persistent disruptive behaviour. At another he was caught – even at his tender age - dealing Class B drugs but his connections saved him. It's all the kind of stuff the shrinks might explain away as attention-seeking. As he got older he discovered the joys of sex. And graduated to seducing female staff at his private boarding school...'

'Seducing female staff? How old was he then?'

'No more than 15 sir. Apparently, he was mature for his age and is blessed with a natural charm that some find irresistable--particularly, it seems, married women. Anyway,

Jason's 22 now and for several years mother and step-father had been buying off angry spouses. Recently, though, their son's found himself a girlfriend. She's called Lisa and seems to have settled him down. They're currently living together in Scotland.'

'Scotland?'

'Yes sir. Jason's part-way through a business studies course at Stirling University.'

Adam gazes at Zoe thoughtfully. 'Hmmm. Despite the redoubtable Lisa, I feel alarm bells ringing. Would Jason, the tearaway with a history of instability, and a sex-drive which compels him to press his attentions on married women, be twisted enough to abduct a helpless child? Have we any evidence, anything at all, which points us in Jason's direction?'

Zoe shakes her head. 'The anonymous caller was certainly not a young man's voice. And we checked out every local owner of Land Rovers and neither Jason nor the Galbraith household showed up in our list. And the skipping rope was found on a road on the opposite side of town to their farm and definitely not the route you'd be driving on to get north of the border.'

Adam drums his fingers on his desk as he thinks. 'Bugger it! I tell you what I want you to do, sergeant. Have a snoop around the Galbraith land. Ask around. See if anyone knows anything about a well. If we come up with nothing, at least it'll show the Coopers that we've taken their request seriously. And then maybe they'll let us get on with our investigation.'

'And if there IS a well?'

'There won't be. But, if by some co-incidence, there is I think we'll pay a lot closer attention to young Jason's movements the night Vicky went missing.'

The following day Zoe pulls up in her marked police car outside the Galbraith farm gates. The country silence is punctuated by a bleat of a distant lamb and the alarm call of a startled blackbird.

Zoe takes a deep breath of the sweet fresh air and quietly muses to herself, 'Now this is more like it. Beats being shut up in an interview room any day. So now, Zo, what do you make of our Inspector Adam Ryecroft? Come on, you can be honest with me. Well..., if you insist...he's good-looking, presentable, got a sharp mind. But for someone with a reputation as a lateral thinker, he seems pretty blinkered. On the other hand you can't blame him for being sceptical. Modern policing struggling to cope with swingeing budget cuts and the Paranormal are hardly natural bedfellows—'

Zoe's introspection's interrupted by a man, dressed in mud-spattered working clothes. He has an East European accent, 'Can I help you, please?'

'Wha...Oh...I didn't see you. I'm just admiring the countryside.'

'You know this is...is...not land for the public? Why police?

'Police? Oh, you mean the car. No, I was on my way somewhere else when I thought I'd take five minutes off, to have a quiet think. I didn't mean to trespass. Whose land is it?'

The farmhand, probably Polish or Latvian, Zoe surmised, replied. 'Land belong to very important man, Sir Francis Galbraith. He does not like strangers.'

'Of course I'll leave immediately. But before I go. Is there a well around here anywhere? You see, I'm a bit of an amateur archeologist – ' Zoe realizes the man's limited English was unlikely to encompass the meaning of archaeologist. 'Do you feed your livestock from a well…you know, hole in the ground.?'

The farmhand shakes his head. 'Animals have water from bath.' Zoe looks at him puzzled. And then realizes he means a cattle trough. 'Where does the water come from?'

'Bath fills on its own.'

Zoe guesses the troughs are linked to the mains and have a valve that operates automatically as the water level drops. So much for the well theory.

She tries one last time, 'And there's nothing that might have been a well?' She gestures with her hands, 'Or, you know, a hole now filled in?'

The farmhand shakes his head. 'No well, water comes from bath.' He looks at Zoe suspiciously and turns his back to her, striding off purposefully. 'Uh-Oh' she thinks, 'I wasn't as subtle as I thought. I reckon Sir Francis will be getting a Polish version of our conversation before I've got back   to   HQ.'

A secretary pauses her dexterous clacking at her computer keyboard. 'Ah, Inspector Ryecroft. Go straight in. The Chief Superintendent is expecting you.'

Adam nods and grimaces. 'Thanks.'

He knocks on a door marked 'Chief Superintendent' and there's a muffled 'come in.'

CS Jack Brodie beckons to Adam. 'Close the door Ryecroft, I don't want the whole of HQ to hear what I've got to say.'

'Sir..?'

Brodie fixes Adam with a gimlet stare. 'Are you absolutely and completely mad, Ryecroft?'

'Sorry, sir..?'

'You flaming well will be...You may reckon you're the bees knees because you've got a law degree and have had more than your fair share of luck. But, that doesn't give you licence to offend one of the county's most respected citizens who also happens to be a personal friend of mind...Not to mention risking making us all a laughing stock with your....I can hardly bring myself to say it...dabbling with...witchcraft in the Cooper case—'

Adams feels the anger rising and his face going red. '-- That's neither accurate nor fair, sir—'

'Oh, so it's not true that you sent Sinclair snooping around Sir Francis Galbraith's land looking for a well, down which some soothsayer claims we'll find the body of a missing child..?'

'I sent Sergeant Sinclair to establish that there is no well A) To eliminate the possibility from our enquiries. But, more importantly, B) to convince the Cooper parents that we're doing all we can – even willing to entertain Dr Wyatt's theories...'

But Brodie isn't listening. 'I can see the headlines now: BAFFLED PLOD TURN TO WITCHCRAFT...COPS IN A TRANCE OVER VICKY...Do you understand what I mean? You're not here five minutes and my force's reputation for steady, reliable, service to the community-- earned if I may say so, by strict adherence to the book-- could be down the toilet because some sharp-suited, smart-arse graduate, wants to make a reputation for himself—'

Adam responds in a firm and level voice. 'Sir, if I may say, your remarks are out of order. The Coopers are at the end of their tether. They're desperate for any scrap of hope. If we're seen by them as refusing to follow up any clue to their daughter's disappearance—from however bizarre a source--they could tell the Press. You can be sure the hacks'll use the information to accuse us of falling down on the job. This way, at least we keep an eye on the Coopers and keep the investigation under our control.'

Brodie is slightly mollified. 'Hmmm...maybe if I explained it like that to Sir Francis, he might understand-- especially if I reassure him that there's never been the slightest suspicion that his farm or his family have any connection with this unfortunate business. He was spitting iron filings over the phone earlier. He wanted your head mate. And making an enemy like him in the Home Office won't help your career, I can tell you.'

Adam goes along with his boss's train of thought. 'I understand that, sir. But I'm sure when you explain the situation to him...'

'Alright, Ryecroft--Adam--I'll see what I can do.'

'Thank you sir.'

'But, from now on, stick to recognised procedures...And don't rock any boats, Eh? A word to the wise and all that...'

Shortly after Adam's uncomfortable conversation he's talking with Zoe as she drives a police vehicle.

'I'm sorry, sir. But I wasn't sure what I should tell the Chief. I had no time to think. He just carpeted me.'

'How did he know in the first place that you'd been up to Galbraith's farm?'

'A farmhand spotted my car. By his accent I think he's East European. He asked me what I was doing and I managed to turn the conversation to how the livestock were watered. I don't think he understood much of what I was saying but he seemed to think there was no well anywhere on the farm. The cattle and sheep all got their water from troughs supplied from the mains.'

'He obviously understood enough to rate you as a suspicious character because he went straight back to his employer to tell him about you and your cosy chat - which has Galbraith so rattled he gets hot-foot on the phone to his old chum, the Chief Super—'

'--Who hauls me in for an explanation after which, presumably, he warns you off...'

'That's about the size of it. And he threw in dire warnings about knowing which side my bread's buttered.'

'So may I ask, sir, now that you're playing this investigation strictly by the Chief's beloved book, why we're on our way to see Dr Wyatt?'

Adam and Zoe are standing on the doorstep of a detached, modern mock-Georgian house. Adam rings the doorbell which is answered by noises of childish excitement. The door opens and a girl aged about six stands there regarding them both with serious eyes.

'Hello, what's your name?' Adam asks. The girl replies confidently, 'Katy.'

'My name's Adam. And this is Zoe. Is mummy in?'

Katy shouts over her shoulder, 'Mummy, it's Adam and Zoe for you...'

Sarah appears behind Katy. 'Adam and Zoe?' She looks at them, 'I'm sorry. Katy's been expecting a friend. What can I do for you?'

'Dr Wyatt?'

'Yes.'

'I'm Inspector Ryecroft and this is Detective Sergeant Sinclair. We're from Wessex Police.' He looks at Katy, not sure whether to carry on. He lowers his voice, as if speaking more quietly might not be so alarming to the child still standing in front of them. 'We're working on the disappearance of Vicky Cooper.'

'Ah...You'd better come in.' _Run along, Katy darling, and play with Daniel a while.' She gestures to the two strangers on her doorstep, 'We'll go to my study, it's quieter in there.'

She shows them into a room with a desk under the window with a large computer on it. Sarah lowers herself onto the swivel chair at the desk leaving two armchairs obviously meant for visitors.

'Please sit down. How can I help?'

'Dr Wyatt, we understand Mr and Mrs Cooper came to see you and you told them you thought their child could be found down a well on land at Avonbourne?'

Sarah shakes her head. 'What I actually said was I thought the disappearance of their daughter might be connected with a well there.'

Adam leans forward. 'What evidence have you got to support that contention?'

Sarah sighs heavily. 'Your idea of what constitutes evidence and mine, are not likely to be the same.'

'Well, to make it easier for us, please assume the evidence I mean is the sort you achieve with painstaking research and forensic science. NOT the kind you get with a Ouija board and a crystal ball...'

Sarah looks at Adam and says evenly, 'What gives me the impression, Inspector, that you're spoiling for a fight?'

Adam plunges on, 'Through your interference in this investigation two parents, already under intense emotional pressure, could be pushed over the edge. And at the other end of the scale, one of the county's leading lights is not best pleased to find his land associated with a notorious child abduction case.'

'Please don't lecture me, Inspector. What I told the Coopers was confidential to them. Who they pass it on to afterwards is their business.'

Adam shoots back, 'But you might have known they'd try to act on what you told them. I regard your actions as thoroughly irresponsible.'

'And why shouldn't they act? After all, the life of their only child's at stake.'

Zoe intervenes, 'From a police point of view, Dr Wyatt, the basis of their information is...well...hardly scientific.'

Sarah turns back to Adam. 'What do you know about the paranormal, Inspector?'

'To me, Dr Wyatt, the paranormal is a pseudo-scientific term dreamed up by people with dubious motives to give a spurious respectability to a load of mumbo-jumbo.'

Zoe says placatingly, 'You have to admit, doctor, the world of the occult does seem an anachronism in the Age of Google, Facebook and Instagram and what have you...'

'On the contrary, sergeant, I believe the occult, supernatural, call it what you will, is more relevant to mankind today than it ever was...You see, the more we rely on science and the more materialistic we become, the more we lose touch with the spiritual side of our natures. This imbalance leads to an un-ease within us. This un-ease becomes dis-ease. Look around you sergeant. Sick minds, sick bodies, sick souls—'

Adam says, 'Now who's lecturing?'

'Sorry. I'll get off my hobby horse.'

'I'm sure I would enjoy debating metaphysics with you one day, Dr Wyatt. But for the time being, can we stick to the Coopers. How can you possibly deduce, by holding a skipping rope, what happened to the child who owned it?'

'At the risk of lecturing you both again I'll just say that some people have the ability to sense certain vibrations given off by inanimate objects. I have that ability. Sometimes I'm able to turn those vibrations into mental pictures.'

Zoe prompts, 'And these mental pictures told you that Vicky would be found in, or near, a well on land at Avonbourne.'

'They told me Vicky's disappearance is somehow connected with a well. And that's what I told the Coopers. I didn't tell them what else I sensed...darkness, fear, suffocation and...death.'

Adam says sardonically, 'For which small mercy we can be truly grateful.'

'Do I assume from your belligerent attitude, Inspector, that Sir Francis Galbraith's somehow heard of my theories and has sent you along to tick me off?'

'Not exactly. Much against my better judgement--but to try to comfort the Coopers in some way--I sent the sergeant here to scout out the land at Avonbourne. Just to make absolutely sure—'

'--And?'

'--And, it was as I expected. According to a farm worker the sergeant spoke to there's no well on the land.'

'I see...' Sarah shakes her head. 'I am surprised. I had such a strong impression...'

'But you were wrong. It's as simple as that. Unfortunately word got back to the landowner who's made his displeasure known to my boss. So, do me a favour Dr Wyatt, If the Coopers ask you to look into your crystal ball again, let me know immediately.' He added stiffly, 'Thank you for your time. We'll let ourselves out.'

Once in the car Zoe turned to her boss. 'Phew! You were a bit hard on her sir. After all, we may consider her misguided, but she was only trying to help the Coopers.'

'Maybe I was, sergeant. But, hopefully, she'll get the message and keep out of police business in the future.'

Back at police headquarters Chief Superintendent Jack Brodie has dialled Sir Francis Galbraith with his phone in speaker mode. After a few seconds the phone is answered.

'Galbraith...'

'Francis...Jack. Just ringing to reassure you that the matter's been dealt with. My new inspector's a sadder and a wiser man. And will be treading on eggshells from now on...' He chortles lugubriously, 'But not around the Galbraith Estate.'

'Thanks Jack. No intention, of course, of interfering in police business. But I don't take kindly to your people tramping over my private land without as much as a "by-your-leave." And, not to put too fine a point on it, if I expect to achieve... er...further elevation in the government, I can't afford to be the subject of any sensational headlines. And you know how the media would just love to get their grubby paws on something like this, innocent or not.'

'Absolutely, Francis. But it won't be a problem. Matter sorted.'

'Good...Er...Incidentally...About that crackpot theory of a well. Are you giving it any credence at all?'

'None whatever. You know me, Francis. I play it by the book. If we get any lead on this kid's disappearance, it'll be through conventional methods not sorcery.'

'Ah, quite so. Absolutely right. By the book. Keep me posted, Jack. Questions in the House and all that...'

'Of course, Francis. Please pass on my best wishes to Rachel.'

'Rachel? Yes, absolutely.'

'And how's that stepson of yours?'

Francis hesitates briefly, which he covers with false bonhomie. 'Oh, doing very well. Not that we hear much from him these days. Found himself a girlfriend in Stirling and she seems to be keeping his nose firmly to the academic grindstone.' He laughs, 'That girl's got more influence over him than his mother or I ever had. Wouldn't be surprised if he moves up to Scotland for good. Anyway, so long as he's happy, eh? And keeping his head down, who am I to complain?'

'That sounds like positive progress, Francis. And now let's hope Ryecroft can give this case a new impetus, eh? It'll be a relief all round when we wrap this one up. The tabloids just won't let it go and they're getting restless and that makes me nervous.'

'Hmmm, I don't like the sound of that. I suggest you pin the abduction of this little girl--what's her name, Vicky?— on someone soonest. Bound to be some criminal with a record of this sort of thing. The public need to be reassured, Jack. Pull someone in quick as you can, Eh? Leave it with you, Jack. Bye...'

Jack looks curiously at the phone as Francis breaks the connection, leaving the room filled with a continuous dialing tone. He muses thoughtfully, 'So, it's over to you, Ryecroft. Let's see you live up to your reputation. But, by the book if you please...by the book.'

The following morning Adam's looking for the third time through the paperwork on the missing girl when Zoe knocks on the door and walks straight in.

'Sir, have you got a moment?'

Adam says ironically, 'Good afternoon Sergeant.' One look at Zoe' face and he regrets the sarcasm. 'It's after ten-thirty, Zoe. Where have you been?'

'Down the local library, sir. If you just have a look at these photocopies...'

She slides several sheets across Adam's desk.

'Yes. Newspaper cuttings. What about them?'

'Sir, they're from the Wessex Gazette. From five years ago. Look at the headlines.

Adam reads aloud, 'MP IN PLANNING CLASH', 'SAVE OUR HERITAGE PLEADS NATIONAL TRUST,' 'MP's PLEDGE ENDS FARM PLAN ROW.' He looks up, exasperated. 'So, local harmony restored. And, since there's acres of small print, can we get to the point?'

'Sir, if you read this opening paragraph...um...just here...'

Adam reads aloud but hurriedly, 'Member of Parliament for Marlborough, Sir Francis Galbraith, has finally settled his long-running row with the planning authorities. After months of wrangling over a proposed development on his farm--a listed building-- on the Avonbourne estate he agreed to keep his scheme within strict boundaries and to use traditional materials in keeping with the character of the seventeenth century structure...' Adam pauses. 'I'm sorry, sergeant, I still can't see—'

'The next bit, sir.'

Adam sighs and reads on. '...Much of the dispute has focused on an ancient well...' Adam's voice transforms into riveted interest. '..an ancient well--also listed--which was considered by the planning committee to be within the curtilage of the property. Sir Francis has now satisfied councillors by promising to incorporate it within his proposed summer house development...' Adam stares at Zoe. 'My God...So there is a well on Galbraith's land...'

'It came to me when I was going over what Dr Wyatt told us yesterday. She seemed so utterly convinced. And then I remembered the planning row. I suppose at the time I must have read about it and it stuck in the back of my mind. Anyway, I thought I'd check the council minutes which are filed in the library...'

'Well done, you. But before we get too excited, this doesn't actually prove anything. Just because we now know there is a well on the Galbraith Estate doesn't give us the automatic right to go stamping our police-issue footwear all over it—'

'So, where do we go from here?'

Adam thought for a moment. 'I think another call on our tame Cassandra might be in order...'

'Sir..?'

'Cassandra...She was condemned by Apollo to prophesy correctly but never to be believed.'

Later, Adam and Zoe are sitting in 'Cassandra's' front

room. Adam is drumming his fingers on the arm of his chair impatiently.

Bill, Sarah's father, breaks the silence. 'Sarah won't be long. The children are just home from school and she likes to spend some time with them then. By the way, I didn't have the chance to introduce myself properly. I'm Bill Anstruther, Sarah's father. We all live together in this house. Unconventional perhaps, but it seems to work. It's not what we would have chosen but after Tom was killed--he was a journalist and got in the way of a sniper's bullet in Helmand—'

Adam says sympathetically, 'So I understand. Dr Wyatt must have found it very difficult...'

'She did, she did. But...well...we all came through...And here we are... Luckily, Tom's insurances mean we have no financial problems and now that I'm retired I can help look after the children which gives Sarah a break.'

'And your family arrangements aren't the only unconventional aspect of your daughter's life either..?'

Bill smiles. 'Ah...you mean her profession. To an

outsider it must seem bizarre. But, suppose I'm so used to Sarah's...er...gifts that I don't think about it any more...'

Zoe joins the conversation. 'Are you a believer then, Mr Anstruther?'

Bill chuckles. 'Let's put it this way...I'm an agnostic. As a maths teacher I became convinced that everything in the universe could be explained with the same remorseless logic of the calculus.'

'And now..?'

Bill sighs. 'And now, the older I get the more I realise how little I know. It's only the young who deal in certainties. As for me I'll opt for the good old Scottish verdict of "Not Proven."'

The door opens and Sarah walks in calling over her shoulder, 'All right, both of you, homework first, <u>then</u> the TV. And I'll be along in a minute to check.'

She turns to her visitors. 'If I could go back through time the one device I'd dis-invent is the wretched television.' She glances at her father. 'I see you've all met, so what can I do for you this time, Inspector? Going to tick me off again?'

Bill gets to his feet. 'I'll leave you all to it...'

'No dad, I'd prefer you to stay. I might need some moral support.'

Adam says, 'Oh, that's all right, Mr Anstruther. In fact it might be useful to have another view. But this is all strictly confidential, of course.'

'Sounds intriguing.'

Zoe says, 'The last time we were here, Dr Wyatt—'

'Oh, please call me Sarah.'

Adam continues, 'Er...Sarah, yesterday I gave you rather a hard time when we talked of a well on the Avonbourne Estate and I'd like to apologise. But your...er...specialism is a bit beyond my ken and I supposed I over-reacted. And, since yesterday, Detective Sergeant Sinclair here has uncovered evidence...er...evidence in the conventional, police sense...that there is indeed a well on the land there.'

A slight smile flickers across Sarah's face.

Zoe says, 'But that puts us in something of a dilemma. Because, we only have your word—'

'What my sergeant is getting at is we'd like you to convince us as you convinced the Coopers... Look, I'll be honest with you both. As you know the Avonbourne Estate belongs to Sir Francis Galbraith, a government grandee and close friend of my own Chief Superintendent. While normally none of that should influence the direction of a possible murder investigation, the reality is...if I institute a full-scale search of the Galbraith farm, I'm putting my neck on the block. So, I've got to be pretty damn certain of my grounds...'

Bill says, 'I can understand your dilemma.'

Sarah says, 'But what more can I say than I told you yesterday? When I held Vicky's rope I was immediately overwhelmed by a sensation of fear...panic...darkness. I felt I was being forced into a confined space. Then more fear...and a terrible loneliness...and then...nothing.'

Zoe interjects, 'But where does the well come in?'

'That was later...I used a form of map dowsing, to fit the

final picture together.'

Adam says, 'Can I get this straight? This is where you hold a pendulum over a map and it tells you things about the area?' He shakes his head. 'A bit difficult to swallow, that...'

'Maybe. But, it works. It's a technique developed by a man called Tom Lethbridge, who discovered that all substances produce what he defined as a frequency or "rate." And he could calculate the rate using the length of a cord between his hand and the pendulum on the end.'

Adam holds up his hand. 'Sorry...you've lost me. This Tom Lethbridge says that everything has a sort of wavelength, depending on the substance it's made of...?'

Sarah smiles. 'Not quite...But you're getting warm. Let me give you some examples: Take silver as a substance for instance. Lethbridge discovered the pendulum would only react by "swinging" when it was exactly twenty-two inches above a silver object. Truffles reacted at seventeen inches, grass at eighteen and a dung-beetle's "rate" was sixteen. Why are you shaking your head Inspector?'

'I'm sorry, but we're back to mumbo-jumbo again. Who in their right mind would believe any of this? And who is this Tom Lethbridge? He's got to be a crackpot.'

'Actually, Inspector, Tom Lethbridge died in 1971. But he was no crackpot. In fact he was Keeper of Anglo-Saxon Antiquities at Cambridge University's Museum of Archaeology and Ethnology. And, in fact it was his studies of ancient religions that led him to make connections between their beliefs and what we would regard today as "other dimensions."'

Zoe tries not to show her exasperation. 'What connection has his theories about pendulums got to do with Vicky Cooper down a well somewhere?'

'Lethbridge discovered something very curious. He found he only had to <u>think</u> of the object and he'd get the same reading. He knew that water's "rate" was thirty inches, so he tried dowsing for water over an Ordnance Survey map and it actually worked.'

Adam blows out his cheeks. 'Now you really are stretching credibility too far. How can you hold a pendulum over a map and find water?'

Sarah says evenly, 'I don't know...but it works. There are dowsers today, Inspector, paid large sums of money by multi-national companies, who use just these techniques to discover oil deposits, gold, diamonds...'

Zoe says, 'This is all a completely new world to me, I had no idea.'

Adam presses, 'So, how did you arrive at the conviction that a well on Galbraith's land holds the key to our missing child?'

'Our Mr Lethbridge also discovered he could get a reaction "rate" for abstract phenomena like light, fire, the colour red and so on...Even death. I've learned to adapt a variation of the Lethbridge techniques. Using a pendulum, I thought of Vicky, at the same time as dowsing a map of the area. The feelings I got were overwhelmingly of death. And these feelings were closely associated with a shaft deep into the ground. And that shaft...I assumed a well...was slap in the middle of the Avonbourne Estate.'

Shaking his head Adam turns to Bill. 'I just don't know what to make of any of this. Mr Anstruther, what do you think?'

'Inspector, earlier I told you I was an agnostic in these matters. But, that doesn't mean I haven't seen some extraordinary things associated with my daughter's work—'

Zoe says, '--Putting it crudely, Mr Anstruther. If your daughter's theory about Vicky was a horse, would you back it..?'

Bill pauses…and then, 'Yes, I would.'

The following day at the Galbraith Estate a heavy doorknocker raps twice with heavy-handed authority. The door is opened by Rachel who looks at her callers imperiously. But her voice holds a note of uncertainty.

'Yes?'

'Lady Galbraith, I'm Detective Inspector Ryecroft and this is Detective Sergeant Sinclair. We're from Wessex police. I have a warrant to search your summer house.'

'A warrant? To search for what? There's nothing there…'

Zoe says, 'Please, Lady Galbraith, may we have the keys?'

Rachel looks over her head to uniformed figures beyond. 'Who're all those people with you?'

Adam replies impatiently, 'They are my officers. You have a well, I understand, inside your summer house?'

Rachel tries to keep the panic out of her voice. 'A well? Yes, but what do you want to know that for?'

At this point her husband strides up behind them. 'What the hell's going on? Who are all those people in the yard?'

Rachel looks nervously at Francis. 'It's the police, dear. They say that want to search the summer house.'

Francis turns to Adam and Zoe. 'Search the summer house? What the Devil for?'

Adam says, 'We're pursuing our enquiries into the disappearance of five-year-old Vicky Cooper, Sir Francis.'

Francis adopts an emollient tone. 'You mean that poor child that went missing a couple of weeks ago? You don't think she's here, surely?'

Rachel fights down the rising fear in her chest. 'He

asked me about our well, Francis.'

Francis is temporarily taken aback. 'The well? Look here, whoever you are what's going on..?'

Zoe explains, 'As we told Lady Galbraith, this is Detective Inspector Ryecroft and I'm Detective Sergeant Sinclair--?'

' --Ryecroft..! But...'

Adam regards him coolly. 'But what, Sir Francis?

'Look here, Ryecroft. I don't know what you think you're playing at but I'm not having you upsetting my wife and tramping all over my home in pursuit of some...some... personal crusade...'

'Personal crusade, Sir Francis? Why would you say that? I'm only interested in locating the whereabouts of a missing child. We have reason to believe she could be over there in your summer house.'

'Reason to believe? You're not serious?'

'Sir, may we have the keys..?'

'No, sir, you bloody well may not.'

'I have a search warrant. If necessary I shall authorise my officers to force an entry.'

Rachel looks at her husband in desperation. 'Oh, Francis.'

'Don't worry, darling. These people will do nothing. Inspector, I demand you stay your warrant until I've spoken to your Chief Superintendent.'

'I'm sorry, sir, I'm not prepared to do that.'

Rachel tearfully blurts out, 'It's no good, Francis...'

'Shush, darling. Just let me handle this.' He turns to Adam and adopts a placatory tone. 'Look here, Ryecroft, can't you see you're upsetting my wife. She hasn't been in the best of health of late--.'

'--I don't wish to cause any distress, sir. The sooner we conduct our search, the sooner we'll be away from here.'

Francis begins to bluster. 'Do you know who I am, Ryecroft? What my position in the Government is? Are you aware of my...er...prospects in the future..?'

Adam replies levelly, 'I know you're a junior minister and tipped for high office, yes.'

'Then you're also aware that I'm a prime target for the muckrakers of the gutter Press. Any hint, any whatsoever, of a connection with a police investigation, and my chances'll be shot for good...'

'Sir, it'll take less than half an hour. If we find nothing, I promise you I'll make it clear to any reporter who might ask that it was just one line of many enquiries we're obliged to follow up and you extended your fullest co-operation. So, now, perhaps you'll allow us access.'

'Damn you, Ryecroft. You'll regret this, I promise you.'

Rachel intervenes. 'Don't demean yourself for me, Francis. Let them do what they have to do. Nothing can stop it now..' She starts to lose control. 'And d'you know something. I'm glad...I'm glad.'

Adam extends his hand. 'The keys, please, Sir Francis.'

Francis's shoulders slump and the fight seems to drain out of him. 'Alright, I'll show you where the well is...We had the architect incorporate it into our Summer house which we had a kitchen installed into so we could use it when we host barbeque parties.' He looks at Rachel. 'You stay here, darling.'

'No, I'm coming with you.'

A few minutes later onlookers are listening to the voice of a police diver giving a running commentary on his descent down the well. There are crockery and cutlery noises as Francis boils a kettle on the hob and pours the water into a teapot. Adam divides his conversation between bellowing down the well and talking across the kitchen to Zoe and Sir Francis and Lady Rachel.'

The diver's hollow voice booms from the well head. 'I'm down about forty feet now, another fifteen to go, I reckon.'

Adam turns to Sir Francis. 'You're sure you wouldn't care to enlighten us on what we're likely to find?'

Francis studiously ignores the question and introduces his own train of thought. 'Unusual, isn't it? I came up with the idea of building a kitchen around the well, making a feature of it, after those short-sighted idiots on the planning committee insisted we couldn't fill it in.'

The diver's voice interrupts. 'I'm at the surface now. God, It's black. It's like ink. Hang on a bit. There's something here...'

Sounds of sloshing, bubbles and spluttering is punctuated by a shout.

'It's a body...'

Rachel gives out a strangled cry of despair. 'No, No...'

Francis hurries to his wife's side and puts his arm around her shoulder. 'Darling...'

Adam shouts down the well, adopting a professional detachment. 'A child's body, Dave? Is it a child's body?'

The diver's voice has a note of puzzlement. 'No, not a child's sir. It's an adult.'

'An adult? It can't be. Dave, are you quite sure.'

The diver's hollow response comes back, 'Absolutely, sure sir. It's too bulky to be a child.'

Adam says urgently to his team, 'Get that harness down

to Dave, quick.' He turns to Lady Galbraith. 'You may wish to go back to the house, Lady Galbraith. It's going to be a pretty unpleasant sight.'

Rachel hesitates and then says resolutely, 'No I want to stay here.'

Adam shrugs, 'Alright, it's your choice.' He leans down the well. 'The harness's coming down now. Strap it round the body and we'll haul it up. Then, go back under and see if you can find anything which might identify it.' And as an afterthought, 'Or a weapon.'

Francis says wearily, 'There's no need for that, Inspector. I can tell you all you need to know.

Amid clearing-up noises in the background as the search and diving team pack away their equipment, Lady Galbraith is still sobbing while being comforted by her husband.

'You're saying the whole thing was an accident, Sir Francis?'

'I've told you, Ryecroft, yes. Rachel and I came home earlier than expected and found the summer house lights on. Jason was here in the kitchen, just standing...clutching a child's toy panda.'

Zoe says, 'And you didn't ask him what he was doing..?'

'Of course we bloody well did. He continued to stand there with this sort of lopsided, almost evil, grin on his face. On the way home on the car radio we heard about a missing child and at first we didn't make any connection with Jason's odd behaviour. But he seemed to be goading us in some way...You may know, Inspector, he's been a...er...difficult boy. Put Rachel through Hell in fact.

'I suppose that's what made me so mad...him just standing there...just grinning. What he'd done to his mother...what a threat he was to my career. It all welled up. Then he was boasting...of kidnapping this child. He waved this wretched toy panda in my face. He said it was easy, as if he was invisible. Nobody noticed a thing. At that I just lost my temper and flew at him.'

'Did he say what happened to the little girl?'

Gulping back her tears Rachel says, 'We didn't get a chance to ask him, sergeant. It all happened so quickly. Francis had his hands round Jason's throat. But, my son just kept on grinning. Then he broke Francis's grip...I jumped between them trying to push Jason away...'

Sir Francis locked eyes with Adam. 'Unless you were there, Inspector, you couldn't possibly understand. The three of us were locked in some ghastly tableau. Suddenly Jason fell back...'

'It was my fault. I was trying to separate them. I pushed Jason as hard as I could...' Rachel voice broke. 'The back of his knees caught a chair and he lost his balance and fell against the top of the well. He tipped over the brink and...and...' She began sobbing pitifully. 'He hit his head on the opposite side...It was horrible...Horrible...'

Galbraith pulled Rachel closer. 'He caught his head with such a crack, Inspector, he must have died instantly. The momentum kept his body going...We heard a splash...Then, nothing. No cries for help, or sounds of struggling. Just silence...'

'So you just left him..?'

'Don't sound so sanctimonious, Ryecroft. Of course we didn't just leave him. I shouted and shone the torch down but I could see nothing. Rachel was in hysterics and by the time I'd calmed her down it was all too late. When we were able to take it in we knew it was him who'd abducted that poor child. The panda proved that.

'And later we found a skipping rope on the chair. We don't know why he took the girl. We could only assume it was for his own, obscene, purposes...Two things we did know: Jason was dead and nothing would bring him back. And, nothing we could do could help his victim...I mean she'd either been dumped by Jason, in which case she'd be found wandering somewhere by your search party...'

'...Or,' Rachel says, 'he'd murdered her and buried her body somewhere. Either way, we couldn't help those poor parents in their suffering...'

'So, Sir Francis, you decided to say nothing. To cover Jason's tracks you made an anonymous call to the police and dropped the skipping rope beside the road to Uffington. Then you hoped your stepson's absence would be explained by a permanent move to Scotland. Eventually, you thought, it would all blow over.'

Galbraith looks at Adam, defeated. 'God help me,

Inspector, that's just how it was...'

A thought occurred to Adam. 'So, what happened to the car Jason must have used to pick Vicky up in?'

'I don't know, Inspector. At first I thought he must have parked it out of sight in one of our barns, but I searched everywhere...and no sign of it.'

Zoe presses, 'So where is it? It's certainly not been abandoned anywhere in Wessex, or it'll have been reported.'

'I wish I knew the answer, but I don't.'

Adam steps forward. 'Sir Francis, I won't arrest you now. But you will have charges to answer like perverting the course of justice and concealing a crime and that's just for starters. There won't be a carpet large enough for you to sweep   this   under.'

The next day in his office Adam is muttering to himself. 'So, Ryecroft, sleeping on it hasn't helped.' He keeps going over in his mind a sequence of events that don't make sense. 'I still can't work out how young Jason got to be standing in the Galbraith's summer house, accompanied by a panda and a child's skipping rope, with no visible means of getting there..? An accomplice, perhaps. But who..? And, why..?'

Zoe puts her head round the door and says urgently, 'Sir.'

'Not now, sergeant, I'm in the middle of a particularly baffling jigsaw. Have you ever tried doing a jigsaw with the key piece missing?'

'But it's not, sir...'

'Not..? What do you--?'

'The key piece isn't missing, sir. We've found her. Vicky.'

Adam looks at her incredulously. 'You've found Vicky?'

Zoe replies triumphantly, 'Alive and well, sir, and living with her auntie.'

'Living with her auntie..?'

'At least that's what she's been calling the woman she's

been staying with for the last two weeks.'

'And the kid's really OK?'

'Right as rain, sir. Apparently, this woman walked into Stirling nick first thing this morning and dumped young Vicky into the desk sergeant's lap. It's a long story, sir, which he told me some of on the phone.'

Adam bangs his desk with the palm of his hand. 'That's fantastic news…where's the girl now?'

'Vicky's on her way back now, accompanied by this auntie and a female police officer. Stirling don't want to be lumbered with the paperwork, so they're saying it's our case, sir.'

'And we're absolutely certain this child is Vicky?'

'Absolutely, sir. No doubt at all.'

'So what the Hell's being going on? What time are they due here?'

'Well, they've already left. They're taking the Glasgow-Heathrow shuttle and I've arranged for one of our cars to meet them at this end. They should be with us by half-one, sir.'

Adam stands and looks at his colleague. 'Well done, sergeant….Well, well, well. No pun intended. But so much for mumbo-jumbo eh. What was it Dr Wyatt said? Fear, suffocation, death...'

'That's hardly fair, sir. After all, a well was involved. And so was a death. And it is_ all connected with Vicky' disappearance.'

'Hmmm. We'll give our mystic doctor the benefit of the doubt for now. More important, what exactly did this desk sergeant   tell   you..?'

Some time later, Sarah is shown into Adam's office.

'Ah, come in Dr Wyatt. You know sergeant Sinclair of course. Good of you to agree to come down to the station...But we wanted to tell you personally the excellent news.'

'News..?'

Zoe says, 'Vicky Cooper's been found, safe and well.'

Adam says light-heartedly, 'But...um...not actually down a well.'

'Found...? That's incredible. Do the Coopers know?'

'Absolutely. There are few joys to be had in this job. But one I shall treasure for the rest of my days - seeing that family re-united again. Look...er...Sarah. In the circumstances I thought you have a right to know what happened. But, strictly on the QT, you understand.'

Sarah looks between Adam and Zoe. 'I understand.'

'Sergeant, as you've now spoken to all parties involved, including the elusive Vicky, over to you.'

'Well, it's a complicated story...make a good serial on the tele...'

Adam clears his throat in admonishment.

'Sorry, sir. It's like this, Dr Wyatt. George Cooper isn't Vicky's real father - Jason Galbraith is. Er...was...He was 17 at the time. He had a fling with Mrs Cooper...a bit of a 'toy-boy' situation, apparently...the result being Vicky. Christine

Cooper made the mistake of telling Jason. He agreed to keep the secret between them. Time moved on and George Cooper believed Vicky was his child. Then Jason decided he needed some money and hit on a spot of blackmail as a handy way to get it.'

'Sarah says, 'So he put pressure on Christine Cooper, threatening to reveal the truth to her husband—'

Adam nods, '--Unless his silence was purchased by a one-off payment of five thousand pounds..'

'--Which, foolishly, Mrs Cooper agreed to.'

Sarah looks at Adam, 'But that wasn't the end of it?'

'Just the beginning in fact. Christine realised he wouldn't leave it at £5,000 so decided to call his bluff.'

Zoe picked up the thread, 'When he started a bit more arm-twisting for another few hundred Mrs Cooper told him to go to Hell. As she'd made up her mind to come clean to her husband anyway.'

Adam says, 'Jason must have realised his golden goose was about to slip through his grasp so he decided to shock

Christine Cooper back to her senses.'

'By kidnapping Vicky?'

'Exactly. But he obviously hadn't thought through the implications. He didn't think of the media outcry there'd be. He just wanted to throw a scare into his erstwhile lover.'

'So, what went wrong? And why have you been talking about Jason in the past tense?'

Zoe looks at Sarah. 'What went wrong was Jason died in an accident. He had a fight with his parents and fell down a well.'

Sarah stares at them thoughtfully. 'A well...On the Galbraith farm?'

Adam nods, 'In their summer house, actually. It used to be a working well in the yard which they incorporated into a self-contained, all mod cons guest apartment, when they modernised the place. Jason turned up there the night Vicky went missing carrying her panda and skipping rope. His stepfather assumed he'd harmed the kid in some way. There was a blazing row and Jason fell into the well, smashing his head on the side in the process. The Galbraiths say it was an accident and forensic tests do seem to support that claim.'

''But where was Vicky all this time?'

Ah...After devising his ill-conceived plan he enlisted the help of his girl-friend, Lisa. According to Lisa, Jason spun her some cock and bull yarn that Vicky was his niece who he'd agreed to look after while his brother and sister-in-law took themselves off for a holiday...'

'And this Lisa believed him?'

'According to Lisa, he was very convincing.'

Zoe continues, 'So, Jason bundled Vicky into the boot of his car---'

Sarah mutters to herself. 'Darkness...fear...suffocation...'

' --Sorry, what?'

'Oh, nothing.'

'...And nobody saw a thing. Later Jason met Lisa at a pub. By then he'd sedated Vicky but Lisa just thought she was sleeping naturally. They drove to the Galbraith's farm, where Jason said he had some unfinished family business. He would stay overnight in the summer house while Lisa took Vicky back in the car to their flat in Stirling. He'd catch the train up the next day.'

Adam chips in, 'But of course he didn't arrive. At first, Lisa wasn't particularly worried... But when she saw the story in the media, she realised she'd been had...'

'...And,' says Zoe, 'was now aiding and abetting a kidnapping. But, she might be stupid but she was also loyal. So she just sat and waited for Jason's return.'

Adam jumps in, 'Meanwhile, Vicky--who'd been frightened out of her wits when Jason had pounced on her-- had calmed down when Lisa persuaded her it was all part of a game. And that mummy and daddy would be joining them on holiday soon. Then she told anyone who asked that Vicky was her niece. The Scottish media weren't very interested in a kidnapping five hundred miles away so it quickly faded from the headlines.'

Sarah says, 'So, there Vicky stayed—'

'--Until it dawned on Lisa that Jason wasn't coming back. That's when she decided to go to the authorities.'

'But, how do you know about Mrs Cooper's fling with Jason?'

'Mrs Cooper herself. When we took Vicky back she broke down and told her husband everything. Mr Cooper's a good man. He said he still loves Christine and Vicky and is just glad to have his family back together again.'

'But why didn't Christine suspect Jason from the start?'

'Christine thought that even Jason wouldn't harm his own daughter. It was only when you mentioned the well and the Galbraith land that she put two and two together.'

Zoe explains, 'But, she thought Jason must be hiding Vicky somewhere on the Avonbourne Estate. That's why she was desperate for us to search there.'

Sarah pauses, smiles and says slowly, 'Well, well, well...all's well that ends well, then!'

Adam replies in mock disgust, 'Ugh.'

They all burst out laughing which is interrupted by the

Chief Superintendent entering the room. 'Well I must say I'm delighted to hear my officers happy in their work...Dr Wyatt, good to see you again. Last time we met was at a reception following one of your lectures—remember?'

'Of course, Mr Brodie. We argued about the merits of inspiration versus perspiration I seem to recall.'

'Well, I was a sceptic, as you know. But all this has obliged me to think again. First, I'd like to thank you most sincerely for the...er...extra dimension your ...insights...brought to the Cooper case.'

Sarah glances at Adam. 'I'm sure the Inspector would have managed perfectly well without me.'

Brodie says fulsomely, 'Nonsense, nonsense. Your contribution led us to a body...And the victim was the key to the case. I've bee thinking...Your...er...special gifts, allied to traditional, police methods, could be a potent weapon against the criminal element. I wonder if you'd consider working for my force on a consultative basis..?'

Brodie gets into his stride and continues enthusiastically, 'You and Ryecroft could pool your talents...Perspiration allied to inspiration, eh? It would certainly give our villains something to think about. You could be part of the team....You could have your own office...no crystal balls though, that would never do...'

A WORD FROM THE AUTHOR:

If you have enjoyed this book please consider writing a review on your Amazon site because this will encourage others to enjoy it too.

And please share your thoughts on social media. If *Cut To The Quick* takes your friends away, even for a few hours, from their stressful lives they'll be grateful to you, as will I.

You may be interested in my other work, which is in a completely contrasting genre. Having gained a modest world-wide following with my books *Dowse Your Way To Psychic Power* and *In Tune With The Infinite Mind* I turned my hand to thriller writing.

If you enjoy escapism look no further than *Ticket To A Killing, The Kirov Conspiracy* and *Kingdom and the Glory*. All my work is available on any Amazon site worldwide - just put Anthony Talmage in the Books search field. I'm now writing my next non-fiction book – how we all have within us the ability to heal.

Printed in Great Britain
by Amazon